ARSENAL

FULL METAL SUPERHERO

BY JEFFERY H. HASKELL

Custom Illustrated cover by:
www.vividcovers.com

To my wonderful wife, Rebekah, none of this would be possible without you. I love you. Also, for Stan Lee, Steve Ditko, and Marvel Comics, thank you for Peter Parker the Amazing Spider-man. You gave a lost boy the precious gift of hope.

ONE

It's one thing to build something and imagine using it. It's another to actually do it.
-From the journal of Amelia Lockheart

Alarms scream in my ears as the ground flashes by, followed by the sky. What happened? Right, White Rhino punched me. Like an idiot, I stood there and took it. My heads up display shows my stupidity in brilliant crimson numbers. Power levels at thirty-seven percent. Kinetic shields— down. If it weren't for those little gems I'd be in pieces all over the pavement.

The narrow streets and tall buildings glistened in the mid-afternoon sun, reminding me I don't have a lot of room to maneuver.

"Epic, re-route power to thrusters and get those shields back on-line!" I didn't need to tell him, not really, he would do it. The light over my boot and back thrusters flip from red to green. I fire them off to give me some control. The momentum lets me stabilize myself and start flying instead of falling.

Amelia, the kinetic shields are damaged.

A list of components and systems scroll across my vision in angry red.

"Now isn't the time for a shopping list. Where's White Rhino and Vixen?" The duo had decided on robbing my little corner of Phoenix. They probably thought the limited number of capes in Arizona made it a prime target. Lucky for Maricopa county I happen to be in the testing phase of my MKI Armored Battle Suit.

I pull up the GPS and put a pin on where they are. Using my hand stabilizers I make a gentle turn, heading back the way I came. My power cells are already recharging under the sunlight. I hit the ground feet first Epic tells me we're at fifty-percent power. Along with my shields, Epic is my other stroke of genius. An autonomous artificial intelligence. Without him I couldn't begin to run the armor.

My kinetic shielding springs to life as the dynamic duo's minions spray me with automatic weapons fire.

I didn't design the suit for aesthetics, but I think it's pretty. Red and white and curvy lines with a slightly feminine look. I am a girl, I don't want to fly around in a man suit.

Epic shows where each bullet hits. My primary invention, the one from which makes entire suit possible, is my kinetic manipulators. Without which, thank god, I would be street pizza.

"Charge IP cannons." I lift my arms up and point my hands out in front of me. Vixen takes off running to the side leaving Rhino and a half dozen flunkies spread out on the street.

The light blinks and I fire. Ionic Pulse energy blasts through the normal humans. The energy overrides the ions in their nerves preventing communications for a few seconds. Not enough to kill them but enough to drop most people. I smile as they spaz on the ground. It's like a Taser on steroids, one which also hits with enough force to flatten a normal human.

Vixen hits from behind, wrapping razor sharp claws around my mirrored faceplate. Sparks fly off her claws as they merely slide along the surface.

The alloy in the suit can take it. I don't know what her claws are made of and I don't care. I grab her wrist and heave her over me. She flips through the air with the grace of a ballet dancer and lands twenty feet away, ready to attack.

My proximity alarm blares. I barely have time to engage my thrusters and leap into the air when a pickup truck passes through the space I had occupied moments before. The truck crashes into the third floor of the building behind me. I wince as the glass and metal fall to the ground.

White Rhino is thirty feet away and picking up another vehicle to throw. I didn't know he was strong enough to do that!

"Charge IP cannons, maximum power!" More alarms as power from my kinetic shielding are diverted to the cannons. It doesn't matter, shields up or down, I can't let him hit me again. I fly up, bank and come back down over the next vehicle he tosses at me. I hope all the civilians have gotten out of the way. I line up for a perfect strafing run and discharge both cannons at near point blank range. The energy blast is enormous and my HUD visibly dims as the drain hits the batteries.

And now I know the flaw of my MKI suit.

He shrugs off the cannons like he didn't even feel them. They literally could take down a real rhino. It never occurred to me I would need a different weapon. Then the world spins as Rhino lands another blow. Alarms scream for a half second then go silent as my power core gives up the ghost.

The G's are too much and I can't hold on. Everything goes black.

TWO

I haven't left my lab in a few days, not since I took the beat down from the dynamic duo. The lab-slash-house has everything I need anyways. I can't believe my shortsightedness. My arm hangs painfully in a sling bumping against my chest whenever it moves. I can't see out of my right eye and I'm pretty sure I have a concussion. Most of these things can be explained away by 'wheelchair accidents'. Even minor ones can sometimes be unforgiving. I would rather not explain it at all, though.

"Epic, play it again please."

Are you sure? He prints out on my laptop screen. I sigh, "Yes, I need to know how to fix this." I have the suit up on a specially made rig that supports each piece and provides power to them individually. If I hadn't hacked the power box attached to the house I could only imagine what my bill would be.

The good news is, physically, the suit is mostly fine. The core frame is forged of titanium bonded with tungsten carbide a mixture of my own design, that as far as I know, isn't possible for anyone else. I don't lightly throw around the word *indestructible,* but yeah, it is. The suit held up spectacularly. With a few added additions, like one more power cell for whatever weapon I come up with to stop people like Rhino, it will be fine. My biggest obstacle to a new weapon system is the limit of my current power cells. I just don't have anywhere to put another one.

The Ion Pulse Cannons work great against normals. It didn't occur to me a super like Rhino would shrug it off.

I glance over at the news as one of the correspondents starts talking about what happened.

"Mute," I tell it. I don't want to hear how a new armored hero had her ass handed to her in three different languages. The good news is, the government spook from the Department of Metahuman Affairs said, 'no comment' and my regional team of state-sponsored heroes, the Diamondbacks, aren't saying anything either.

I don't think they would have fared much better. Rhino is unbelievably strong. The public database has him listed as an F4. Which explains why he could toss a truck at me without breaking a sweat. I spend a few minutes programming a link for Epic to download the database and compare it to news stories worldwide. The next time I go into a fight I want to know what my opponents are capable of.

I'm still annoyed about them escaping. His last punch sent me a mile away. By the time I returned they were long gone. At least they hadn't gotten away with very much money.

As I'm tinkering I notice the Diamondbacks are on screen Investigating the scene of the robbery along with the police. Their leader, Major Force is moving some of the rubble of the vehicles like it was made of paper.

I'm glad there isn't an APB out for me because the suit and I aren't ready. I pull up a hologram of the internal workings and look for a way to route more power to the shields without blowing—

A pebble hits my window. I try to ignore it, but it is followed by another one.

"Amelia," I hear from outside. I sigh and roll myself over to the window. Carlos waves from below, grinning like an idiot. Fortunately for me, he's the only one who knows my secret. We've been friends since I moved into the neighborhood, four years ago after I finally achieved emancipation from my uncle. Carlos was the only kid who would come talk to the girl in the wheelchair. I think I can trust him, besides if he was going to betray me he would have a while ago.

I open the window and stare down at him. My brow furrowed, "I'm busy, come back later."

"Holy hell, what happened to you?"

"You didn't see the news?" I say.

"That was you?"

I nod, "Now, go away, I have work to do."

"Come on, bring me up and let me hang out. My brothers family is over and my house is way crowded." His older brother has a wife and four kids. Carlos' parents had a decent spread on their children if I recall Juan is about forty. Carlos, like me, is twenty. He should be in college or working, instead, he spends his nights playing guitar and his days sleeping. That is when he isn't over here watching my flat screen TV and drinking my Cokes.

"Fine, I'll buzz you in," I tell him. I live and work on the second floor. I had it seriously customized, including having the front door run on magnetics, allowing me to open and close it from up here. I hate having to go up and down stairs. Even with a lift, it's a pain in my rear end.

He looks disappointed. I know what he wants but I'm not doing it. The sun is still up and I can't risk anyone seeing him float up into my workshop.

I remodeled the entire second floor to be three rooms, a workshop, my sleeping slash entertainment room, and a large bathroom designed specifically for me. On top of all of the comfort modifications, I added thermal resistant paint, a Faraday cage, and reinforced the walls with enough carbon steel it would take a tank round to punch through them.

I hear him knock downstairs and I wave my hand at Epic to have him open the front door. A few seconds later he is in the room rummaging through my mini fridge for Cokes.

"I don't understand why you don't patent this stuff and retire. You could make a mint, set yourself up at Encanto Park, have a driver, live the life of a rock star." That would appeal to him. I can't help but grin.

The process by which I bind the alloys together would net me millions, maybe billions, but money isn't my plan. I do need some for my research, but my goals are much further afield than mere dollars.

"I need to get this right and then I will think about all of that," I wave my hand, dismissing the idea. He's never asked how I could afford everything I have. I think he is under the impression I inherited the house or something. I don't have the heart to tell him I sold an inertia absorbing energy oscillator to Lockheed when I was fifteen. It's how I afforded the house and the lawyer to emancipate myself from Uncle Inezo.

In the meantime, I started a trust for my poor Uncle. It pays for his counseling and for a sponsor to encourage him to go to his AA meetings. He has no idea. He's not a bad fellow, but he isn't my mom and dad. He was just the only relative who would take in a six-year-old with a broken back. Maybe he did it for the check, maybe not, I don't know. At least he took me in, the rest of my family sure didn't.

The money I made off the deal left me with a little over twenty million. It wasn't hard to create a company, I call it Mars Tech Global, a lofty-sounding name. Technically I am the sole person on the payroll. I'm also the CEO. I use the company to order my parts and then route them to my house. It's all very complicated, but it works, mostly because of Epic. Of course, I put him to work on trading algorithms and he's busy making me money from the money I have. Money may not be the goal, but it certainly makes things easier.

"But how do you afford all this stuff? This place looks like you robbed a computer store from the future."

I smile, "Just because I won't sell the suit doesn't mean I won't sell anything. Hand me that scanner will you?" He passes it to me and I run it over the suit one more time. Even a microfracture could prove fatal. The suit has to have full structural integrity to work at peak efficiency.

"So," he says as he pops open a Coke, "What went wrong?" He gestures to the screens showing my fight with White Rhino.

"I made one weapon and thought it would cover every eventuality. It didn't." I say with a sigh. I need another weapon on the suit, but how do I get past the power requirements? I can maybe add one more power cell, making the total three, but even then I don't know if it will be enough to mount another system. As it is I have about four hours of light activity, two of moderate, and thirty minutes of sustained combat. Adding the extra cell would only give me maybe twenty percent to those figures. Assuming I can even figure out how to add it.

"Amelia, take a break, the suit isn't going anywhere." He turns on the Xbox and fires up our favorite game, "Besides, I need some payback for the other night."

I let out an exaggerated sigh. He's right, the armor isn't going anywhere and trying to fix things on a tired, beat-up brain isn't going to help.

"Oh come on, Carlos, you think you can take me? Pshh, not on your best day could you ever come close to me on my worst day."

"It's on girl. It's on like Donkey Kong."

I push my wheels over next to him and pick up my own controller. I have a custom one with my name on it, as does he. The game is exciting and pretty quick I lose myself in our verbal sparring.

"No wonder you lost your fight, you can't hit for crap," he jostles me in the shoulder.

Then I headshot him. He goes still for a second before he mutters *dammit*. I will give him this, in our mixed culture down here, guys do not take well to losing to girls, especially macho guys. Carlos though, he lets it roll off him like water off a duck's back.

"Okay, niña, round two."

I envy him. My mom was a first generation immigrant from Columbia. She and dad met while they were in school and they hit it off. However, I never really learned her culture or language before...

Carlos blasts me and my avatar goes flying. The game spins around in the death slow motion allowing me to see my rise and fall in perfect detail.

While we're waiting for the next match to load he leans back, "Your super Tasers didn't work against him, huh? Too bad, you can't shoot him with a rocket or something. Of course, he's built like a tank so that probably wouldn't help."

I close my eyes and try not to sound too sarcastic, "You think?"

"He's not like you, though, right? I mean he has to punch you or throw something at you... what if you could just," he snapped his fingers, "make him float away?"

I slap myself in the face. I'm an idiot.

"Why didn't you come over earlier?" I tell him.

"I have to time my moments of genius for maximum effect." We laugh.

He isn't wrong. I can build a grenade launcher and use my pods as a ranged weapon. I rub my hands together. It will take a little work, but I think it will be awesome.

THREE

The grenade launcher is pure genius. By collecting small amounts of my exhaust as I fly, I'm able to put a pod, or anything similar in weight and size, almost three hundred feet away. Now I can arm it with any combination of weapons. I had to add a few pieces of telemetry to Epic's algorithms and now he can account for any weather condition when I'm firing. Not that Phoenix is ever anything other than hot and dry.

This high up my power cells recharge as fast as I expend them. I can also see the city of Phoenix laid out before me like a big gray lake nestled in between mountain ranges.

Carlos certainly wasn't wrong. If it was money I wanted, I could make a fortune selling all my tech. It's not though. I want my parents back. I shuffle those thoughts away, they're painful and I don't want to deal with them right now.

"Epic, show me news and/or footage. Keywords 'crime in progress' 'powers' 'Rhino or Vixen.'"

The list of searches flies by. Epic knows to filter out the useless garbage and also the things erroneously marked with today's date. Two things pop up. One's an amusement park and the other is a bank.

"Why an amusement park?" I ask my AI. The possibilities pop on screen. It's a long weekend, the parks will have a larger till than normal. The police response time would be slower as well. I think on it for a second. The other article is the police increasing bank security around National One, the largest bank in Phoenix. If I were Rhino, I would go for the park.

"Plot a course for the park," I tell Epic. My faithful AI brings up a GPS overlay. At two hundred MPH, I can be there in under five minutes. I dial my thrusters up to max and bank for the west.

I can't feel the air against my skin, but the suit buffets like mad, even with its friction-light coating. I feel the little plates on my shoulders and back shifting to compensate for air flow while the computer does its best to keep a non-aerodynamic form flying. With my arms out wide and slightly behind me, the two main flight stabilizing thrusters keep me level, while the rest work to keep me pointed in the right direction.

When I first designed the suit I had no idea getting the human form to fly would be this hard. It's a wonder Supers like Protector and Aeon can do it with their powers, let alone go as fast as they do.

I have two unfulfilled goals with my suit, supersonic flight, and a really big gun. Something powerful enough I could punch through a battleship. I think I have the defense covered. Between the kinetic shielding and the alloy of the actual armor, I'm pretty sure I can survive anything. At least once I find a way to amp the shielding up. Probably not a nuke, but almost anything else. I'm pretty sure your average criminal doesn't keep nuclear weapons lying around.

The map says I'm thirty seconds out when Epic pings me. Footage from Youtube pops up showing Rhino barreling through the main ticket stand at Enchanted Island while Vixen takes down the guards with her usual grace. The way those claws sparked off the suit, I can only imagine what they would do to flesh. I hope none of the guards are dead, but I can't see how they wouldn't be.

Being late and having people die because of it puts my priorities in place. When I return to the workshop I'm going to find a way to increase my speed. Until then, I bring up all systems and charge my shields and weapons.

I hit the concrete with a ground shaking landing. Little spiderwebs run out from where my feet hit. The suit isn't actually heavy enough to do anything like that. Landing with my thrusters going does. I'm going for awe factor here. I bring up both my arms with my palms out.

"Rhino, Vixen, STAND DOWN," Epic makes my voice much more authoritative than it would otherwise be. It also broadcasts in fifty decibels. Not enough to damage hearing, but enough to get their attention.

They laugh.

"You up for round two, tin-girl? Well then, get ready." Rhino's thick New York accent is almost too much to understand. Him stomping his feet and scratching at the ground isn't. They can't see my smile through the smooth silver faceplate. Vixen continues loading cash into what looks like a backpack made for someone as tall and large as Rhino.

The ground shakes as the twelve-foot tall behemoth charges me. Each foot fall shatters the concrete beneath his feet. It isn't really his fault if I recall right. A government program to create super soldiers running in a federal prison did this to him. I don't know if he was this messed up before, but he certainly is now. His skin is alabaster white and thick as a tank. His feet resemble telephone poles and his body is three times as wide as a normal human.

Epic calculates he's moving at thirty-five MPH, perfect. The grenade launcher flips into place over my right shoulder. Targeting cross-hairs spring to life and overlay Rhino's chest. He must think I'm scared stiff for not moving.

"Fire," I say. There is hardly a noise as the pod flies through the air. The six-ounce piece of metal impacts his chest an instant later. I've got it covered in a lightweight epoxy which explodes on contact, sticking it to his chest. The light clicks on letting me know it's active and suddenly Rhino lifts up.

I wave at him as he stares at me incredulously from twenty feet up. With no weight and only friction to stop him, Epic estimates he will go several miles before halting.

The park guests smartly stay back, but I hear gasps and mutters of glee as Rhino is removed from the equation.

I turn back to Vixen, expecting her to attack. Instead, she's running.

"Thrusters, charge IP cannons." The suit takes off and I direct it through the air. I can do a pretty good job at speed where velocity can carry me through mistakes and I can push off the wind resistance. At low speed, the suit isn't maneuverable at all. Vixen, on the other hand, is like a world class gymnast who decided to take up parkour and juicing. I have one shot before she's gone.

"Epic, full power cannons, proximity shot, fire when ready." I lift both my arms and point my palms directly toward her. It's hard to do while flying because it pulls my stabilizers offline and I have to sort of hover. Both cannons fire. The sound they make is somewhere between a battery suddenly discharging and sandpaper on wood.

I'm flipping backward and my breakfast threatens to come up when I crash into the ground. The kinetic shielding reduces it to nothing more than if I had fallen while standing, but it shakes me up.

"What happened?" I ask groggily. Epic shows me the math. At full power, while sustaining the most difficult form of flight, the energy from the cannons, which is usually nullified by my forward momentum or me standing on the earth, was enough to spin me in the air and then into the ground.

"Duly noted, no cannons while hovering." Yet another issue to deal with. If there were any way to have my hands free during flight, save having wings, I would do it. I don't want wings. I did a design with them and it looked awful.

"Did we get her?" I ask as I pull myself up.
Unknown.

I resist the urge to dust off the suit. I pull up the full sensor suite and scan for Vixen. I annihilated the fence she was leaping over, but I missed her. Great.

"Epic, are paramedics inbound?"

Affirmative.

I hope they're in time, but there isn't anything I can do. I ignite my thrusters and head off in the direction of White Rhino.

He's easy enough to find. The pod carried him up a thousand feet and nearly two miles away. Air currents must have grabbed him at some point. It's good to know. If I forget to collect someone with these they would eventually suffer from hypoxia and die. I make a mental note to add air traffic control access to Epic. That should cover weather and any planes. I'd hate for a 737 to crash into something I'd podded.

He's spitting mad when I get to him. I picked up some rope on my way and lasso his foot, then I tie it to my waist and ignite my thrusters. He has no weight, but boy, he has wind resistance. Flying while towing him is all but impossible. The problem is the local police can't handle him. I have to drop him off at the Buckeye State Prison, almost thirty miles away. To make matters worse, I can't slow down without him crashing into me. It's going to be a long trip.

He curses at me the whole way. When he starts describing how he is going to violate me I turn off my external feed. Intellectually I know he can't, but the emotional person inside of me doesn't. I hadn't thought about the consequences of catching criminals. What they would do and say when they were caught, or if they ever got out. All the reason to never, ever, tell anyone it's me.

I'm breathing heavy from the exertion when I pull us to a stop over the Buckeye yard. Their alarms are blaring and I see AA cannons popping up from hidden turrets. I can't imagine they receive a lot of flying guests who aren't here to break someone out. I hold up my hands and ignore the alarms on my screen showing targeting vectors. Suit sensors pick up scattered radar and infrared beams trying to lock onto me. Good luck with that. If they do fire I'll just pull the pod on Rhino and fly off.

They don't fire. On the tower nearest me a door opens. A Hispanic man in his fifties dressed in a nice suit steps out. He is all smiles as he walks to the railing closest to me. He reminds me of my father a little bit, and the beating my heart has already taken today increases a little more.

Epic's automated process does facial recognition on him through the Internet. His picture, along with a complete bio pops up. My preprogrammed algorithms put him at a trust level of over seventy percent based on all available data.

"Hello," he says politely. I decide to take a leap of faith and shakily maneuver next to him and land. Well, fall less than gracefully. I almost make it without going to a knee. When I recover I catch myself smiling at him. He has an infectious personality. He can't see my face.

Epic modulates my voice when I speak, I sound nothing like me. "Warden, I'm sure you know who this is. Do you have a facility I can put him in?"

"We do... I'm not sure who you are, though?"

I ignore the question; I don't have a name yet and I'm terrible at coming up with them.

"Can you take charge of the prisoner?" Listen to me speaking all cop talk. He smiles at me again. Even in the armor, I'm not imposing. End to end I'm five-six. The armor adds two inches bringing me to a whopping five-eight. My under-suit is formfitting, it has to be, but the armor is bulked up in areas to give me more protection. I end up looking a little bulky more than svelte. I can't help it, components take up space. I can't have a one-nano-meter thick armor and have anything in it. I need inches.

"Okay, play it coy if you like, but I'm trying to help. The DMHA is going to come calling and what I tell them can either hurt you or help you," he says. I'm not the only armored person flying around. There are at least a half-dozen heroes and villains who use armor. Most of them have superpowers of some kind. I've researched them all. However, you don't have to have superpowers to fall under the domain of the Department of Metahuman Affairs.

"Tell them I'm not a meta-human," I say, trying to sound more confident than I really am. The DMHA is the one group I don't want to tangle with yet. If they don't think I have powers it may buy me a little time.

"Okay, if that is how you want to play it," he sighs, "Drop Rhino over there," he points at a pit opening up. By now Rhino had calmed enough to handle. He still gave me the death gaze as I pulled the pod. He falls thirty feet down into the hole.

Once I know he's secure, I wave at the warden and activate full thrusters. I watch the prison shrink behind me on my HUD.

"Okay Epic, plot a course for home. Can you order a pizza from Bianco's?"

It's Friday.

"Right, okay, well pick one of the others I like. I need a little me time and some Star Trek."

Affirmative.

FOUR

I glance at the UHD TV I keep on the far wall. Rhino is being moved to the super-max prison in North Dakota today. It's the only long-term facility capable of handling him. Apparently, he has stamina enough to slam his head against the wall over and over for several days. Even the strongest concrete would give after a while. I'm not too worried about it because the Diamondbacks, Arizona's premier super team, are on hand. I don't have any sound on, which is good. I need to focus.

I still don't have a solution for my flight stability problem, but I think I came up with another weapon. My kinetic shields absorb energy and then dissipate it from my suit's vents. Essentially, it ends up being converted to heat energy and then wasted. I can use it to power something else. I'll still lose about thirty percent in the conversion when it is all said and done, but I will have one more weapon to add to my arsenal.

I can fire the kinetic force beam from my head by adding an emitter. It's easy enough and it is what I'm delicately doing now. It's a perfect weapon, not unlike my grenade launcher. It is completely powered by absorbing energy being used against me. The only downside is If I want to do more than a strong shove, I need to be hit hard. I put the last piece into place and carefully solder the line. I'm working at a magnification strong enough to see nanometers. Even the slightest movement could hurt the process. I hold my breath until the computer gives me the okay.

I put the helmet back on the field which holds it in place. Epic runs his diagnostics and it is time to take a break. I'm sweating hard enough I need a shower. I run a comb through my shoulder length black hair. It used to be longer, but anything past my shoulders doesn't fit in the armor. The armor has to be as snug as humanly possible or I could be seriously hurt by even a minor shift in velocity.

Thirty minutes later I finish drying off and I'm back in my chair. I feel ten times better.

The TV flashes a Parker alert. The code they use when telling civilians to be careful of superhuman activity. I don't have to read it to know what it will say. Someone is trying to break Rhino out of jail.

I grab my synth suit and pull it on. It's a struggle while sitting in the chair. Normally I would lay in bed and do it, but I don't have the time. The black material covers me like a glove and allows me to interface with the neural links in the suit. It's what allows the armor to respond to my nerve impulses. I move like normal and the armor responds with the same amount of speed as if it were my own limbs. It's what allows me to walk even though I'm paralyzed from the waist down. Essentially, the suit acts as an external nervous system, bypassing the damaged ones in my lower back.

Once my black leotard is on I roll under the pull bar and line up the chair with the marks on the floor. The bar lowers to where I can grab, then it pulls me up.

"Epic, initiate," I order. The AI complies, the armor flies off the wall as one piece and wraps around me like a second skin. The whole process takes less than ten seconds and my HUD boots up.

"Show me the action, I want live footage." The prison is forty miles away. At top speed, I could be there in twelve minutes. I don't even bother to shut the skylight as I blast away. I accelerate as fast as I can. The wind bangs me around as the computer tries to compensate.

The pip pops up letting me see the fight from the reporter's point of view. The Diamondbacks are seriously outclassed. It isn't Vixen alone trying to free White Rhino, but her, dozens of men with guns, and four supers from the wrong side of the tracks.

"Identify threat levels," I command Epic. His main housing is back in the workshop. There isn't any feasible way I could put the necessary components to run him inside the suit. We use tight beam UHF radio for most of our work. He can also track me through the Internet and keep logged in. Hacking most wireless signals takes him less time than it takes to say, 'wireless signals'. This way the computer housing he lives in can be supercooled back at the house. Plus, with him not in the suit, the power requirements are far less than they would be otherwise.

The four villains pop up on my screen. My timer says I only have a few minutes to figure these guys out. Frostfire is categorized as the most powerful. The database says he's an F4. He can generate fire and ice blasts and has limited control over the elements. He uses the ice as armor and his fire to keep himself warm while doing it. I may need to take him out first.

Grappler is your basic strong guy. He's not as strong or as invulnerable as Rhino, but he's agile and can fight.

Tess Harper, a telekinetic who can form shields, there isn't a lot of information on her. She doesn't even have a codename.

Finally, there is Deadman, a gun-toting lunatic who is determined to rid the world of super people. A real Psychopath. It is unclear if he has superpowers or if he is just highly skilled.

Time's up. I can see the battle ahead. A large military style transport with a flatbed has Rhino strapped in place and likely sedated. The Diamondbacks are pinned down. They don't really have any heavyweights. It's not like people want to be in Arizona when they can pick somewhere else. Major Force is their physically strongest guy, the other two have more utility powers.

Frostfire has the soldiers pinned down with gouts of flame. Grappler is going hand to hand with Domino and Mr. Perfect. Domino can teleport and fight, Mr. Perfect is a so-called 'mage'. Vixen is trying to cut through the straps holding down Rhino and Harper is—I slam hard into something and deflect straight down. I put my arms up and yell as I crash into the ground. Dirt and sand cover my display and play havoc with my sensors. I must have hit one of Harper's shields. My heart thumps in my ears making it hard to focus.

I push myself up only to be slammed back down. I didn't realize she could use her powers like a battering ram. The kinetic shields are holding but she's still putting enough pressure on me to override my own strength. I watch the power cells drain noticeably.

"Epic, maximum horizontal thrust!" I can only imagine the blast of dirt and sand behind me as four thrusters go to full burn at once. Will this even work? I slip past her telekinetic barrier and am free in a second. I spin around, flying backward, I scan for her.

"I think your categorization of threats might need work." The good news is my kinetic force beam is now at 100% power. Someone is going to have a bad day and I think it will be Harper.

The suit's sensors ping her. She's standing behind Frostfire, an ice shield slowly melting in front of her. Frostfire has two streams of flames like mini tornadoes spewing seventy feet in front of him. The soldiers are all face down in the sand trying to stay under it. I don't know how long they can last, but it won't be long. Lives come first. The DB's are going to have to handle Grappler on their own.

"Charge IP cannons, maximum yield area effect." Shooting them over an area diminishes their capacity, but it will get attention. I need to be less than thirty feet to use them. I put my head down and bank around. Epic does the calculations for me and I decide another header at two-hundred miles an hour isn't a good idea. My shields are still recovering from the first one.

I brake hard and come down to highway speed. I'm flying right at them and they don't see me—

Epic fires for me. The Ionic Pulse charge spreads out and smacks into them. They both scream. Would it be enough to knock them out? Harper falls immediately. Frostfire turns his attention to me. I smile. This is going to be good. I land twenty feet away and pipe my voice over the PA.

"Surrender now and you won't have to go the hospital." I don't know where I come up with these lines, god they have to sound cheesy.

"Funny," he says. Fire leaps from his hands and splashes against my suit. The shielding is ineffective as fire is heat energy. However, my titanium tungsten carbide armor won't even be warm to the touch until he starts turning sand to glass.

"Lock on with Kinetic Lance," I think of a cool name for it as I say it. I like it. Epic brackets him and I grin again.

"Fire." I watch as the invisible beam of force strikes him in the chest, sending him flying. The flames die immediately. The HUD says the air temp is eight-hundred degrees and I don't feel a thing.

"Charge cannons, fifty percent power—fire." I flatten Harper with another stun blast to make sure she's out and follow up my lance on Frostfire with a third stun blast. They're both out. Which leaves Vixen, Grappler, and Deadman.

Bullets ping off my armor as I stride past Frostfire. Epic puts a diagram on my screen showing me they're seven point six two millimeter rounds. They're powerful rounds, capable of penetrating most armor. But my suit isn't just anything. Maybe if he had a fifty-caliber sniper rifle I *might* be worried.

Deadman takes a knee next to the truck Rhino is on and he's firing what Epic identifies as an AK47. Brass spits out the side and I'm pretty sure every round hits. I flinch for the first few before I dial up my kinetic shields and watch as the Lance charges and the bullets stop in mid-air. They fall to the sand a foot from me. He may be a nutjob but he's persistent. He lets his rifle drop on its sling and pulls his pistol. He fires as he moves to the left. He's heading for cover. Epic brackets him with the lance.

"Fire." The invisible force shoots out and sends him spinning into the car he was going to use for cover. I spread out my hands and blast him with the cannons to make sure he's down. His spasming body tells me he is. I spin around for whatever is next. Vixen is floating in midair, purple bands of energy are wrapped around her. Grappler is being dragged unconscious to the back of the truck by Major Force, the team's leader. He's six four if he's an inch, short blond hair, and crystal blue eyes. Epic lists his powers as strength, agility, and a preternatural danger sense. It doesn't say super good looks because even my scientific heart melts when he looks at me.

I just wish he wasn't scowling.

"Who the hell are you?" he points his finger at me.

Uh-oh.

Unconsciously I look around. He can't be talking to me? Then he walks right at me and I realize he is. Did I screw up some secret operation? I saved lives here.

"Listen," I pipe over the PA, "I put Rhino in the hole and I wanted to make sure he stayed there. It looked like you could use some help, so I helped. You have a problem with that?" I cringe inside, I shouldn't have said the last part. Apparently, putting on this armor ups my sass factor.

From the way, his eyes narrow it's obvious he does have a problem with it. He looms over me. My armor adds a few inches but not much. I'm liking him less and less as the second's tick by. Is he going to punch me? I'm pretty sure I could take his whole team down but that would screw up my plans. This isn't going at all like I wanted.

He looks like he's about to yell at me when Domino places a hand on his arm and pulls him back.

She fills her costume like it was poured on. Her mask, half white, half black, like her name, covers the area around her sparkling eyes.

"Luke, she helped us out big time, try not to blow a gasket. Go talk to the First Sergeant and make sure all the men are okay," she says. Interestingly, I notice she leaves her hand on his arm the entire time. His demeanor shifts and he nods.

"Okay fine, you talk to her."

I take a step back if they plan on attacking I need to flee, not fight. We watch him go and she turns her smile to me. She's a pretty woman, green eyes, black hair, tan skin and she certainly is fit, like a cheerleader from a movie. I wouldn't know what one looked like in person, I never went to High-school.

"Don't mind him, once a marine always a marine. I'm Domino, what's your name?" Her tone is pleasant and comforting.

Warning, atmospheric toxins detected, switching to internal air supply. Twenty minutes remaining. The red clock flashes at me while I watch it tick down. Normally I wouldn't need compressed air to breathe. I built the suit to filter out most things and auto-switch me to internal when needed. The warning happens when Epic thinks I might be in dangerous air which cannot be filtered.

Is she emitting some kind of mind controlling pheromone? Is that why Force stood down the way he did? I realize she's still waiting for an answer.

"Cat got your tongue? Or do you not have a name?" Her smile is all white teeth and red lips. Even after the obvious effort she undertook to bring down Grappler, she doesn't have so much as an eyelash out of place.

My back bristles a little at that. I grasp for the first thing in my head, "Arsenal, I'm Arsenal." She nods. I have to admit it isn't bad, and I have been adding weapon systems and I do plan on a few more, there are worse names I could have come up with.

"You know, doing this sort of thing," she waves around at the villains, "requires training and a license. Technically I should ask you for yours since this is a government operation."

I knew this would be a thing, and I'm ready for it.

"As you might have guessed, I'm new to all this. I believe I fall under the sixty day grace period?" I reply. It's in the law, it's supposed to cover people whose powers express and they haven't figured out if they want to be a costumed hero or something more normal. Of course, I don't have any powers, only my suit.

Her eyebrow shoots up, "Oh, you sound like you planned this out pretty good then. Do you have an idea of what you are going to do next? I think we could fit you in on a probationary status if you need a sponsor."

I must have impressed her if they're offering me a spot on the team. I do the mental math on my timetable. I was planning on spending at least a year making a name for myself. I could go with the Diamondbacks now, but would it help me? Or hurt me? She mistakes my pause as hesitation.

"Listen, we're not as strict as we let on. The DMHA may have authority, but it is mostly for show. We're not government employees. Technically, we answer to the governor of Arizona first and everyone else second."

She pulls out a small card from somewhere and holds it out to me, it has a domino mask on it, her name, and the address of their HQ.

"Swing by tomorrow afternoon and at least check the place out. We've got a pool..."

I nod as I take the card. I have nowhere to put it. I look down at it for a second.

"Epic, record," I say to him. He flashes a picture from the two-gigapixel cameras I built into the helmet. I really don't have anywhere to put the card, I clutch it in my hand until I can toss it.

Turning the PA back on I address her, "I will, three o'clock okay?"

She nods.

Without further conversation I ignite the thrusters on my boots and surge into the air. This has to be my favorite part of the armor. If there was a way to experience the wind against my face, it would be even better. However, if any part of the armor is detached, the whole thing suffers. I can open my faceplate, but I lose the neural link if I do so. I let the card fall from my hand when I'm a half mile away. I wouldn't put it past them to try and track me. Which is why I took off in the opposite direction I came from.

An idea hit me like a lightning bolt. I need stealth tech. Why hadn't it occurred to me before? I shake my head, for a smart person sometimes I'm really dumb.

Now I'm on the radar, quite literally in fact. Alarms go off as my electronic warfare suite detects the radar waves bouncing off me in different directions. Right now my cross pattern isn't too big, but with some modifications, I bet I could make her invisible.

I angle my arms up a little more with the palms facing up while cutting speed. I slide down slowly. The altimeter on my HUD sinks to three hundred feet before the radar warning light goes off. Good to know the movies have it wrong. They always say five hundred.

Rows of houses and lawns pass underneath me as I wake up the dogs with my thrusters. Until I install sound bafflers there isn't a lot to be done about the noise.

Since I'm already thinking about adding systems I should also consider a more powerful weapon. Everything I had worked great in the last fight. Looking over the telemetry I notice the kinetic lance lost more energy in the conversion than I had calculated. I dislike the idea of lethal weapons, but I might have to put at least one on the suit, for emergencies.

Now if there was only a way to cram another power cell into it...

FIVE

Staying up all night to design a new power cell to fit around my hips wasn't the brightest thing I could have done, especially since I was meeting the new team today. I wake with drool on my cheek and the side of my face is numb from where I fell asleep on the desk. I stretch to work out the kinks. It had to be nine or ten, I never sleep in past—it's two-thirty.

Crap.

I shuck my clothes as fast as I can. My foot gets caught on my jeans and I end up struggling with them. Hurry it up Amelia. It never ceases to amaze me how I can change clothes every day with no problems, and then when I need to do it in a hurry, they find a way to be stuck on the chair. Deep breaths calm me down. I look at the calendar. This could move everything up by *years*. My synth suit goes on next. It's considerably easier to put on, I must be getting used to wearing it. The front seals shut from crotch to neck and once the seam hits the top, it melds in the reverse. With it complete, it is a one-piece suit which will only come off if my hands, or Epic takes it off.

The armor flies off the rack and wraps around me like a second skin. Sadly, the new innovations will have to wait. For now, it's the same old, same old. The HUD lights up as Epic loads my OS and does the preflight to make sure the seal is solid. I get the green light and I'm gone, blasting into the air right out my skylight which closes automatically behind me.

They have their base in North Phoenix, about twenty miles from my house. I head east at three hundred feet cruising at two-hundred MPH for four miles before I bank hard left, slow down to one-fifty and glide up to eight-hundred feet.

My arms are sore from all the flying I did yesterday. The suit might make me marginally stronger than I am normally, but I still have to fight the air to maneuver in any way.

On course now, it gives me a few minutes to think. If I join the Diamondbacks, how likely am I to be noticed by the national team? According to all my research, the Brigade is the team who works the closest with Category-7. My father's former employer and the company responsible for ruining my life. Normally I try to push these thoughts aside, to focus on the mission. Not today, today I need to look at it with a clear head. I pull up the newspaper article from the worst day of my short life. I know some would laugh and say, "How can a twenty-year-old girl know anything about pain?" Fourteen years ago next month, My parents were taken from me.

My father worked for Category-7, the largest contractor for the government run super teams. They build containment devices, run the Ultramax in North Dakota, they even provide the hoverbikes most of the non- flyer's on the state militias use. They have their fingers in everything.

My dad loved his job, I remember that. I was six when we went on a surprise vacation to Southern California. We were driving along Pacific Coast Highway when a tire blew and our car went over the cliff. I faded in and out for two hours, but at some point, men in uniforms with Cat-7 badges pulled my parents from the wreckage. Why they left me, I don't know. When I woke up in the hospital every doctor, nurse, and person I saw, told me the same thing. Both my parents had been killed. It was a tragic accident, no one was responsible. I was six and from that moment to now everyone I've ever known, with the exception of Carlos, has lied to me about it.

In the end we buried two empty caskets. Uncle Inezo was the only family member who would take me in, mom's older brother. His drinking was a problem, but other than that he was nice enough, when he was conscious. He lied to me too, he would tell me they were dead and I just had to move on with my life.

I'm crying in my helmet, which is a real problem, I can't exactly wipe my face.

"Epic, make note, I need to find a way to wipe my face. Lasers maybe?"

Note made. Amelia, I recommend not using lasers to dry your tears.

"It would be awesome, but yeah, you're probably right. I should also work on synthesizing a voice for you."

Addendum added.

The plan is simple then, join the Diamondbacks. Use them to infiltrate Cat-7, find out what really happened to my parents. Make responsible party pay for it. I'm not the government. I'm not a crusader for law and order. I'm a daughter with an astronomically high IQ who wants her parents back. I may have missed out on my childhood, but if I could have them back, it would be worth it.

SIX

I'm not sure what I expected the facility to look like when Domino handed me the card. A mansion maybe? A sprawling HQ with manicured lawns and gate guards even. I'm sure it's on TV all the time but for the life of me I can't remember ever seeing it. What I found was a three story brick building from the 1920's, a skylight and helipad. Outside is a modest parking lot with a couple of vehicles in it including a dark red Ford truck that looked well cared for. This didn't exactly scream superhero HQ.

I'm glad they keep it close to the city, as I come down to land the sudden change in position leaves my arms aching. I resist the urge to rub them as I cut out my flight gear and land with a thump on the center of the *DB* emblazoned on the helipad.

They have their three hoverbikes parked to one side, a skylight and a large metal door with a keypad next to it. I expected a welcoming committee or something. Nothing. I walk over to the door and hit the buzzer next to it.

"Yes?" A bored voice asks.

"Um, Arsenal to see Domino," I say in my synthesized voice. I feel like an idiot saying my name out loud. I know the world of superheroes has flashy costumes and cool code names and I need to get used to it if I'm going to be part of their world, but it still feels silly. People tend to freak out if the guy next to them shoots laser beams out of his eyes and his name is 'Bob' and he's wearing the same clothes they are. The costumes keep everything grounded.

"Use the button marked 'office-2', please," he says without further explanation. The door opens and an elevator waits for me. There are five buttons, 2-4 are marked *office,* then ground floor, and the bottom one is red with no marking and a special biolock next to it.

The lift shakes and creaks as it carries me down. Underwhelming is the word that comes to mind. Last I looked the DB's received almost six million from the state, and another four from the Feds, along with however much the private sponsors kicked in. Where is the money? Certainly not in this rundown, old, rickety building. The lift comes to an abrupt halt and the doors slide open. The floor is carpeted and the walls are painted with the soothing off-white color no one actually likes. It doesn't look rundown, but it certainly isn't ten million dollars nice.

"Epic, passive sensors on full, I don't want to show them my active sensor suite unless I have to."

Understood.

There are six doors on this floor. I don't see any others and the space of each of the offices would account for the total square footage of the building. Are they hiding something underground? The offices are easily the size of my workshop. The first one has *Major Force: Team Leader* in gold on the door. Team leader huh, he has that painted on his door. Maybe he is more of a pompous jerk than I thought. Too bad about how he looks, those abs alone would make me forgive a lot. I shake my head, no time for that. Only the first three have names, Mr. Perfect and Domino are on the next two. I see she has the corner office.

Domino does the teams PR and is the public face. She's pretty, charismatic and always seems to have the press on her side. Even when they completely muff it up. It gets me thinking about the environmental toxins Epic warned me about. She must have some sort of empathic influence, maybe she doesn't even know she does it?

Domino's door opens, and to my surprise a blonde woman who looks exactly like her smiles at me.

"Arsenal, you came! Looks like everyone owes me twenty bucks. Come on in." She gestures into her office. It's nice inside. Plush leather couches, a full picture window seated to catch the rays directly, and an entire wall of expensive flat screens. Each one has a different news station, all are muted. I carefully walk to the center of the room and look around. I'm not sure where to sit when she points at the couch. As I sit she drags a small ottoman over and sits directly in front of me.

"It's my secret identity."

I cock my head to the side.

"The hair. It's how I keep my identity secret, and a pair of glasses." She fishes out a pair of thick black glasses and puts them over her face.

"Seriously?" My synthesized voice loses some of the sarcasm but she still picks up on it. It's not possible her disguise could work...

"You would be surprised. Of course, those who know me well aren't fooled, but the general public? They aren't looking for Domino in Kate Petrenelli. Marketing manager by day, superhero by night," she says with a grin. The ease in which she puts me is almost frightening. However, the moment she started talking the toxin alarm went off.

"Domino—"

"—Kate, please."

"Kate, I have an internal air supply, but it's finite, can you turn off your pheromones, or is it unconscious?"

Her eyes grow wide as a plate when I speak. For a second I think she's going to be angry then she starts laughing. It's like bells and chimes, everything she does is perfect.

When she's done she wipes her eyes, "Yes I can turn it off, let me hit the fan." She doesn't move, but I sense she gives a command because an exhaust fan kicks in from somewhere. Within seconds Epic turns off the alarm. I'm off the canned air for the moment.

"You know, I've talked to a lot of supers and not one of them could ever tell. I forget about it myself sometimes. It's just part of my power set."

I nod, "It's okay, I didn't think you were trying to be malicious. I didn't even know if you were aware you had it." I say. This is getting awkward fast. I want to cross my legs, or lean back but the armor makes the first impossible and the second would have me looking almost at the ceiling. I need to work on flexibility.

"Epic, make a note to look for ways to make the armor more flexible." I say to him, not her.

"Well, I'm glad you came. There's a lot I would like to show you today, if you would like. You can store your armor here, or you can do whatever you normally do with it when you take it off."

It hadn't occurred to me they would want me to take it off. I look down at my legs. Without the armor I can't walk. I didn't bring a wheelchair, not to mention I don't really want to reveal my face to them yet. If I tell her I need a chair, it will narrow down the list of who I could be considerably. There aren't a lot of raven-haired paraplegics running around. No pun intended.

I decide to go with a version of the truth, "The armor requires specialized equipment to put on and take off. I'm afraid I can't do it anywhere I like," I say to her. To Epic I say, "Make a note about—"

Mobile armor removal, understood.

I giggle, he knows me well.

"Oh, okay, well I think we can make an exception this one time. Let's get started." She pulls out her phone. With a punch of a button a hologram leaps out in front of me. Smart is an understatement for what I am and I can't make a hologram work outside the controlled environment of my lab. She has a mobile one...

"These are our standard non-disclosure agreements. Anything you see here is for your eyes only. It isn't to be discussed with anyone, posted on the Internet, put up on a vlog, or in your diary. Understood?"

I nod.

"Sorry hon, I need to hear the words. It cues in on your voice."

"Oh, I understand and agree."

"Excellent," she says with a smile as she puts the phone away.

"Can I ask a question?" I know it makes me sound like a child, but I feel like one at the moment.

"Sure, hon, you don't have to ask to ask."

"Who made the tech you use for holograms? It isn't commercially available, heck, as far as I know there isn't anyone close to a working version of what you just did."

She smiles coyly, the kind of smile that says 'I have a secret', "Well, if you join the team we can answer that question, until then you will just have to guess. Now, follow me please. And no active sensors or we'll have to ask you to leave."

I do follow her. If I could get a glimpse of the inside of the phone, even an x-ray, it could give me a clue as to how they have tech like that. We return to the elevator, I give it a dubious look as she ushers me in. She places her finger over the scanner, "Main hall please."

The elevator starts down. After it hits the basement the ride smoothens out.

"This part is going to feel—a little weird."

I open my mouth to ask her what she means when my suits master alarm screams in my ear. All my passive sensors light up like Christmas. There is an agonizingly long second where I want to respond and give Epic orders but I can't speak. A light fills the elevator and then it is gone. The doors open and she walks out, smiling as if nothing happened.

"Epic, status report, what was that?"

He doesn't respond. Oh crap.

SEVEN

"What just happened?" I say out loud. My voice always sounds weird to me, but now it's muffled without my PA. No Epic, no control of the onboard systems. Thankfully the synthsuit doesn't require an active interface, it amplifies my existing nerve impulses.

Kate smiles at me from a room that doesn't belong in the building above. It is sleek and modern looking. The outside of the lift is a shiny metal with no visible buttons. I walk out into the room and realize this is a cafeteria. Several people mill about eating and talking, maybe a dozen in total. Some in costume, others in the bright yellow coveralls of Category-7.

Oh my god, we teleported, that has to be it.

"Well, I can't really tell you—"

"—Unless I sign up, don't worry about it. I guess I'm going to have to get used to technology that doesn't exist, like quantum teleportation." Her mouth drops open and I get the feeling she isn't surprised often.

"How did you know?"

"Maybe I'll tell you if I sign up." I keep forgetting to speak louder. My voice ends up being muffled instead of awesome. She nods, her eyes narrow on me as if she is re-evaluating her opinion.

After a moment she leads me to the room and shows me the large kitchen, it looks like a five-star restaurant with everything I could ever want. There is a long line of food, drinks, even several cooks in the back.

"This is a lot of food for four people."

She laughs, "Since you figured it out, you should know this is the ultra-secret HQ for the entire western United States. We have six speedsters on the left coast and they can literally eat a cow after a mission."

I nod. This is starting to make sense. Why spend the money individually when you could pool it. All the teams are linked slightly anyways. If not from members by the fact they're all state-sponsored militias. My mind reels at the possibility. I start doing the calculations for the amount of energy the quantum teleporter uses. I'm so involved in it I follow her on auto-pilot.

Epic hasn't come back and unless they have a Ethernet port I can jack into—I blink a few times, I got lost in my own thoughts and didn't hear anything she said. Major Force is standing there next to her, in civilian work out attire. He's a little sweaty and he's using the towel around his neck to pat himself dry.

"I'm sorry, I am a little speechless from all this."

He smiles, "Listen, about yesterday, I wanted to apologize. I can be a little intense during combat due to my powers amping up with adrenaline and I can get a little cranky—"

"—That's an understatement," Kate interjects.

"—No commentary from the peanut gallery, please," he says with a smile. "Anyways, I'm sorry." He holds his hand out. I take it and his grip is as solid as he is. He still towers over me but I regain a little of my respect for him. I'm glad I'm in my armor, I would hate to have him see me blushing. Focus!

"Well, you know," I say awkwardly.

"Okay big guy, let me show the lady around some more before you start scaring her away with your chiseled abs." He suddenly lets go of my hand and turns away quickly. I catch a glimpse of him blushing. Wow.

The tour goes on from there. She shows me their quarters, the command center staffed by a dozen workers in Category-7 jumpsuits, and a comm center manned by more Cat-7 employees.

"I didn't know Cat-7 was as involved with the teams as this." I try to say casually.

"They contract with the government to provide the majority of our services, from tech like my phone, to our merchandising. Some of what they do they earn a flat fee from the Feds, the rest is paid by the states and their percent of the merchandising. Last year my collectible figurine outsold everyone's but Princess Panther."

I cringe at the name, "Do you ever get tired of the code names?"

She smiled, "You get used to it. Some of us, the ones who are more—how shall I say—pleasing to the eye, make quite a bit of a bonus every month from our toy sales and appearances. It's even a bit of a competition on the sly."

I knew merchandising was a big deal, I just didn't think it mattered much. Apparently I have a lot to learn. Good thing for me I learn fast. Learning is good, but what I really need is Internet access to check in with Epic. His emergency protocols probably have him hacking NASA by now.

I follow her along as I scan for one. This place is a marvel of engineering, it's obviously underground, but without going active I have no way of knowing. She continues the tour to their recreation room. State of the art computer terminals, TV's with headphones, even cots for sleeping fill the hall. Carlos would love this place. Since this seemed like the time to ask, "Do you guys have Internet?"

She points, "We have all the cool toys. We're plugged directly into the backbone which gives us incredible speed. Go ahead and look around for a minute. Bear in mind, you get daily access to all this if you join up," she says with a sly smile. She moves away to speak with a nondescript man who walked in while she was talking. I try to look casual as I check out the computers. State of the art and then some. I had no idea. I thought I would have to work my way to the national team to have this much access. I'm in the heart of the beast. I guess this settles it for me, I'm going to join. Now, I need to let Epic know where I am. It's easy enough to reach behind and unplug the Ethernet cord from the nearest computer. Once my armor's electromagnetic field makes contact I have instant access.

Why are you in Oregon? Epic asks me.

The suit's HUD springs to life and suddenly I am back in control again.

"Epic, I need you to write a quick program to give me voice access to everything. As soon as I let go you won't be able to connect to me."

Wireless?

"I don't want to open the suit up to prying eyes."

I need three minutes.

While he does his thing I flip through the passive sensors to see what's going on here. My ECM master alarm blinks to life immediately. Someone is shooting x-rays at me, along with fluctuating magnetic fields, infra-red beams and a kitchen sink or two. A smile spreads on my face. As far as I know, nothing can slip between the molecular bonds of my titanium—tungsten carbide armor. Nothing. All they will get is an outline. However, I pick up a lot. The air is climate controlled and lacks any impurities, which means it's likely canned.

Another man enters the room, he's wearing a white lab coat and carrying a tablet. He keeps glancing in my direction while I fake my interest in the computer. A radiation warning pops up. Which is odd. If we're underground the only radiation I should detect, outside the x-rays they're bombarding me with, would be background.

"Epic, analyze wavelength."

I can't.

"Why not?"

While my passive sensors can 'see' it, the wavelength isn't one I have on record. I cannot tell you what it is, because it doesn't exist.

"Damn," I mutter. The HUD blinks and he notifies me he's done.

"Don't risk detection but learn everything you can about this place."

Affirmative.

I put the cord back in and Epic immediately disappears. His subroutines stays and I have full control. It would be a little less responsive but it would work. The warning lights die on the ECM, but the radiation warning remains. It piqued my curiosity. The tech I had seen so far was beyond the current commercial ability of any country I knew of.

"Arsenal, this is Sam Carver, he's our chief technical officer for the West Coast, and this is Pedric Matahal, he's the—person behind a lot of our tech and VP of the company. He's here visiting, I thought you would like to meet them since you seem interested in technology."

Carver tripped all over himself to shake my hand, "It's a real pleasure to meet you—uh—Arsenal. Can I ask you a few questions about your—uh—armor?"

"You can ask, I won't promise I'll answer."

Matahal was next, the man freaked me out. His eyes were cold as he stared at me. He didn't blink, or smile, as far as I could tell he didn't have one emotional reaction to anything. Other than to sneer a little when he touched the armor.

"What is the coating you use on the outside, it seems to be resistant to standard wavelengths?" Carver asked.

"I designed it that way on purpose. Technology in the wrong hands can be dangerous, don't you think? What do you use to power this base?" I did some quick mental math, "What do you need, one point six trillion BTU's a day?"

That got a reaction out of Matahal.

"You can't possibly know that, you just pulled that number out of your—" he growled. Kate smirked like I said something funny. Maybe she liked the guy as little as I do.

"Like I care if you believe me. I'm right though," I say.

"1.7, you are very precise. Would I be correct in saying you designed and built your exo-suit?" Carver asked. Uh-oh, I guess I already committed to this.

"Yes," I say.

Both the scientists look at each other and they argue without speaking. Finally Matahal nods to Kate and leaves without a word. Carver turns the tablet he's holding around in his hand a few times before wiping his forehead.

"I have to apologize for my associate, he's not used to—"

"—Being civil?" I fill in for him.

"Quite. Can I ask, how is it you can run your exo-suit and generate as little heat as you do. Thermal imaging puts you at a degree under body temperature."

"Is it Doctor Carver?" I ask.

He nods eagerly.

"Okay, let's tit for tat. You show me the power generators here and I will answer any one question you have about my suit." I don't think they will go for it. I'm sure they have tech more advanced than mine. Heck, for all I know they can teleport me out of my suit anytime they want. Of course it would require a sensor lock... and how did they do it in the elevator? Some form of 'always on' field?

"I don't think we're authorized to do that—" Kate starts to say.

"—Nonsense, this is just as much my base as yours. I have the clearance, I will authorize it," Carver says. Kate raises an eyebrow at him and shakes her head.

"Alright doc," then to me, "Arsenal, I will leave you in his capable hands. When you're done have him page me and meet me by the elevator. Enjoy the show."

After she is gone Doctor Carver practically leaps with excitement as he leads me to the power room. I can hear him mumbling under his breath what he should ask me. Poor guy, I bet he doesn't see tech he doesn't understand very often. To be honest. I know how he's feeling. Quantum Teleportation? Who has that?

The room he brings me into looks like an interrogation chamber from a police drama.

"We can't actually enter the room the zero-point field is in, but you can see it from here." He reaches over and pushes a button. I'm reeling from his revelation. Zero-Point field? Quantum mechanics isn't even close to understanding—

The light comes on in the other room. Floating in the center is a canister no bigger than my hand. It glows slightly and my passive sensors tell me this is the source of the mysterious radiation. I open my mouth to speak but I can't find the words. Zero-point... it's no bigger than a car battery and it powers this base? I put my hand to the glass to feel if there is any heat. Passive picks up... room temp. As far as I can tell the other room is completely survivable.

"Our bargain?" He asks suddenly.

"I can't believe you have this, I mean I see it, but... still working on believing it." Then I realize he was looking at me expectantly.

"Right, sorry doc, you could have shown me an alien and I would be less stunned. Go ahead."

He wipes his brow and I can tell he's eager. "What is it made of?"

It really is the only question he could ask. Everything else is easily guessable. However, this is my baby. I smile, at least I know he will appreciate the response.

"I found a way to bond Tungsten Carbide to Titanium molecules."

Now it's his turn to be stunned.

"H—how?" he stammers out.

"Trade secret. I can't have an army of these running around," I say. Like I would tell him anyway. I spent half my life building this thing to find the truth of what happened to my parents. What these people *did* to my parents. I'm not going to give up my one advantage.

"I guess you wouldn't. Still, bonding Titanium... are you a metallurgist?"

"I'm a lot of things. One of them is protective of my identity. There aren't a lot of metallurgists with PhDs in the world. I answer your question and it won't be hard to find out who I am."

He nods. It's not like they aren't going to know soon enough. I have to join if I want to find out the truth.

EIGHT

It's been two weeks and I haven't given them my answer. Domino offered me probationary membership. It's a big deal. They have no probate members at the moment. I would be the only one. Considering they have two empty slots to fill, I would be a fully fledged member in no time.

That's the problem. I'm still not sure I'm ready to tell them who I am. It never occurred to me Cat-7 would be as involved as they are. If I join, I will have unfettered access. It shouldn't take Epic and I long to find them. On the flip side, they will *know* who I am. They'll know I'm the daughter of John and Hope Lockheart. I'm stalling in the hope of finding a way to fix this... well, that and I wanted more time to come up with the answer to the zero-point equation.

I wheel over to the glass I use as a chalkboard to take my mind off this. It is low enough I can reach it top to bottom without much effort. I've tried these calculations seven ways from Sunday, none of them work. This may be the first time in my life I haven't been smart enough. There is simply no way to make a stable zero-point field. None.

"Whatcha working on?" Carlos asks from the window. He crawls through and flops down on my bean bag.

"No, by all means come in, you're not interrupting anything." My sarcasm flies right by him. He reaches over and opens my little fridge and pulls out a soda.

"I'm trying to find a way to stabilize a quantum field so energy is both infinite and finite in a given space, at the same time. I don't think it can be done. I know it can be done. I just don't know how."

"Infinite energy, that would power the hell out of your suit." He takes a long pull from the Coke. Now I'm thirsty. I wheel over to the fridge and grab one of my own. Caffeine helps me think.

"Yep. Pretty much." I needed it too. I added a particle beam to my ever expanding line up. Only on my right forearm. It will cut through hardened steel. I consider it extremely lethal. A last ditch for a super out of control, or if I have to cut something away in a hurry. The problem is I have to shunt all power to it. No kinetic shields, no IP cannons, nothing. Not only will it take all the energy I can produce, it will sap my batteries. I estimate a thirty-second recharge cycle. If I use it, I better make damn sure it's the last thing I need.

"You going to join them?" he asks as he takes another long drink.

I heave a sigh, I have to, I don't want to. I like Domino, of course I think everyone likes her. "Once they know who I am it won't take them long to figure out who's daughter I am. They took my parents, they're going to suspect something."

"I've never asked, niña, but... you were six? Are you sure it was them? What if everyone was telling the truth, as painful as it sounds. Mira, it doesn't seem likely everyone including your family would lie to you, does it?"

I've been over that moment in my head a million times. I know the psychological effects of reliving a trauma and how an incorrect memory can seem real. Even more so than an actual memory. Am I crazy? Did I imagine what happened?

I look down at my hands. I remember. I remember him taking them and looking me in the eye and telling me I would be okay. It wasn't a dream, I wasn't unconscious, it happened.

"It happened, Carlos, I know it did," I say finally.

"Too bad you're not Carlos Rodrigo Dominguez. I think every Hispanic from here to Columbia is named Carlos or Rodrigo. Can you fake your identity?"

It's a thought. One I've given a lot of weight too, however, Epic says it won't work. I shake my head, "According to Epic, it won't hold out for anything past state level. There are sealed databases even he can't get access to. Once I sign they will run background checks and it will reveal the truth. Better to go in as me and be ready."

I wheel back over to the suit. I've poured my heart into it. I run my hands along the rough exterior. The only smooth portion is the quarter moon shaped faceplate. I could have made the whole thing smooth and shiny, but it didn't seem like it would look right. I'm glad I didn't. The shades of red and white really give it a versatile look. Not too dark, not too light. I grin, okay it is bad ass looking.

"You admire that thing too much, niña."

"You could be right. Well, I'm not going to accomplish anything more tonight. Stay for a movie?" He smiles, "Why do you think I came, your TV is way better than mine."

It's a good movie, sci-fi, one of my favorites. Star Trek never gets old. I can't focus on it, though. My mind wonders back to the ZPF equation. Without something more, I don't see how it could work. Obviously their understanding of Quantum mechanics is greater than mine. At the same time, it can't be. It's a finite field of study, there is only so much to learn and once you have it all, the only place to learn more would be at a place like Cern with a particle accelerator. I've read every book, every paper. This isn't the first time I've thought of zero-point energy.

They did it. Somehow it is possible. If it's possible for them, by golly it's possible for me.

NINE

Phoenix isn't exactly a bastion of super-powered criminals. Patrols are four-hour shifts taken twice a day. As a probationary member I must be followed by a full-time member at all times. I accepted a week ago and after the forms I had to fill out relieving them of obligation if I die, and the training videos, I was allowed out on patrol. On today's patrol it's Mr. Perfect. He's a nice enough guy but he talks almost nonstop. Ask him one simple question about his energy constructs and he won't shut up about his *magic*. As if hem isn't another creation of the Wardenclyffe incident. Yet, somehow, he is among a group who claim they aren't. They're special, they can do *magic*. They're special allright, just the kind you treat with medication.

"When I twist my hand this way, and say *Ectal-muhabeny* it gets really interesting." He stops long enough to take a bite of his hot dog. This feels surreal to me. We're standing downtown surrounded by skyscrapers and he's sitting on his hover-bike, eating a hot dog while I stand against the wall with my arms crossed.

People stop by every few minutes to have their picture taken with Mr. Perfect. Cars honk their horns at the magical man and drivers wave. A few look at me but I haven't made the news yet, they don't even know my name. As he smiles for another shot I can't help but wonder if he named himself.

"Perfect, Arsenal, we have a possible sighting of Vixen downtown, your HUDS will have the exact coordinates," central chimes over the radio. Mr. Perfect has an earpiece, I tuned in one of my receivers to the right frequency. A red pip popped up on my HUD. Epic creates a least time route for me instantly. Mr. Perfect acknowledges the call, takes one more picture with a very pretty Japanese woman and then hops on his bike. He blasts off on the anti-gravity tech they used for the members who can't fly. I put my arms straight down with my palms at a forty-five-degree angle and light off my thrusters.

"Epic, let's shunt power to the Kinetic fields, I don't want any surprises."

Affirmative.

The lights on my cannons, life support, and every other non-critical system dim. It would mean I would have to wait a few seconds to charge my IP cannons, but it also gave me 100% shielding.

It might be overkill, as far as we knew her crew was still in lockup. As far as we *know*.

"Federal Marshals have been notified and have their own agent en route, call sign Bricklayer." Epic pops up a small window with his stats. Typical fed, all strength.

Mr. Perfect acknowledges them while I focus on flying. We didn't have far to go, I throw my hands out in front of me to counter my thrust and set the armor down next to a row of tables sitting under the kind of mist sprayer everyone uses to stay cool outside.

I light up my whole sensor suite. The canyon-like walls of the city limit the range I can 'see.' But if she's near, I'll have her.

"Epic, tap into local traffic cams and see if you can't spot her."

He pings acknowledgment on my screen. Hacking isn't easy for him, it increases the chance of being detected. However, a good first patrol wouldn't go unnoticed. Also, I wouldn't mind having a killer like Vixen off the street. The quicker I can get on the main team—

A piece of lead a half inch wide and almost two inches long blasts through my kinetic shields and hits me square in the face plate. My head snaps back and I'm seeing stars as I stumble backward. Pain blossoms in my stomach and I feel like I've been punched. I scramble back trying to find something to cover myself. My kinetic shields are offline and my HUD is blinking in and out of existence. The area around me glows with a pink hue. I blink away the stars and I see Mr. Perfect standing over me, waving his hands in complicated patterns forming a shield.

"What the hell was that?" he asks.

I don't know. My HUD reboots and Epic is back in full control. There is a scratch on my faceplate. Un-freaking-believable.

"Can your shield stop a fifty caliber sniper rifle firing tungsten penetrators?" I ask him.

"Hell no. It *can* keep them from seeing you. Whoever is firing that kind of ordinance isn't likely to blind fire."

I nod. No, not likely.

"Epic, do you have a twenty on the shooter?"

Affirmative. Two miles due east, on the roof of the Park building.

"He's two miles to the East. Holy hell, who could make a shot like that?" I ask Mr. Perfect. He shrugs.

"Okay, hold the shield, my batteries are recharged. I'm going to take off and hit him. You follow as quickly as you can." He opens his mouth to argue but stops himself. I can imagine he doesn't want to get hit by one of the rounds.

I nod and hold up my hand, three, two one. Thrusters blow the debris and dirt from around me as I shoot up into the air through the glass of the outdoor cafe. I hope the Diamondbacks insurance covers that. I don't want to have to write a check for it.

"Epic, show me the math."

A string of calculations flash to life in front of my eyes. Whoever made this shot is either the best shooter in the world, or someone with super powered help. I divert all power to the kinetic shielding. No doubt the only reason I'm still alive is because I had full power to them when I landed. Tungsten penetrators? Why would the shooter load armor piercing rounds?

The roof appears from behind the last building and I can see him; he's dressed all in black, with a ninja mask and a hulking sniper rifle shouldered. The barrel alone had to be three feet long. He brings it up to bear on me. I don't want to risk another hit. I swerve hard as fire leaps out of the barrel. I don't have time to aim, I eyeball with my kinetic lance and fire. The concrete roof in front of him explodes. He flies through the air to land on his back ten feet away. The rifle rolls from his hands to clatter against the pebbled roof.

"Charge IP Cannons, fifty percent."

They light up green as the man jumps to his feet. He draws two pistols so fast it was like I didn't see him move. Each one spits out twenty rounds. The shield absorbs all their energy and the bullets drop harmlessly to the ground.

"Who are you?" I demand in my synthesized voice.

"Help me, please," he replies. Help him? He's trying to kill me. He drops his pistol and pulls out a grenade. It might cause collateral damage but—he runs straight at me.

My thrusters flare to life and I'm airborne.

"Epic, why did you—"

Below me the man screams as the grenade bursts to life. It isn't explosive, it's thermite. A fountain of white fire burns into the air like a kids firework. The grenade engulfs him in orange flame. His screams of agony fade as the chunk of charred meat that used to be a human being falls to the rooftop.

I guide myself to land. My heart thumps in my chest and my stomach feels like it's in trouble.

"Open faceplate," I gurgle. It opens a second before I spew vomit on the roof. I drop to my knees and heave again. I try not to look at the puddle of molten metal and flesh that used to be a man. That could have been me. Titanium melts at three thousand degrees. Thermite burns at four thousand. I vomit one more time, the last of my breakfast coming up. I can't stop the shaking as I roll over onto my back to look at the sky. The faceplate slides shut a few seconds before I hear the whine of Mr. Perfect's hover bike.

"Holy shi—what did you do?"

Between the tungsten rounds and the thermite, this sure feels like it was directed at me.

TEN

"You sure you don't want any time off?" Kate asks me. We're hanging out in her office, not the hidden HQ. She says she prefers the quiet and none of the guys from the California team can hit on her if she's not there. I'm pretty sure she means Triple Threat. He's three copies of the same person. The only difference is their powers, strength, speed, and flight.

"No, I'm good, I think. I've never seen anyone die before. Let alone as horrible—." I shake my head as the image of him burning to death haunts me. I desperately want to take the armor off suddenly, but I've still found no way to do it without my equipment at the workshop.

She's sipping a diet soda and looking out the window of her office. "I'm really sorry, I can't imagine how awful it must have been. I don't know if it will make you feel any better, but I've been there. My first year out I was in the field when a F4 strong man beat up his girlfriend. We had more members back then. It took the whole team to subdue him. You think an F4 is only a little more powerful than a F3 like Luke, but no. It's exponential. The coroner's office had to scrape her up with shovels." She shivered as she spoke.

She's not the only one, I can't make my hands stop shaking. I still can't understand. Why he would kill himself as a last ditch effort to kill me? I've put exactly one person in jail, and I'm pretty sure Rhino wasn't behind this.

"Any ideas why he was trying to kill me?"

She cocks her head to the side and raises an eyebrow at me. "What? Oh, no honey he... was a psychopath. All Deadman wanted was to kill every person with powers he could get his hands on. He's murdered dozens of F1's. You just happened to be there. He could have just as easily gone after Pierre." Something about her theory didn't sit right with me. If *any* super would do, why load armor piercing rounds? Why have a thermite grenade? He carried practically the only two weapons on Earth capable of hurting my armor.

"What's an F1, anyways? I thought it didn't start counting until three?" I ask.

"Normally we do. F1's can't do any real property damage. They have passive powers or useless ones. Since the Wardenclyffe incident in 1903 there have always been those who aren't as... *blessed* as you and I."

"Kate, I've told you, I don't have super powers."

She smiles like I'm trading an inside joke with her, "Well until you get out of the armor, the boys in the lab aren't going to believe you. They all think you're mentally controlling the metal, or you're some kind of sentient construct."

I would say those things are crazy, but we live in the kind of world where all of it is possible.

"I've heard of people with powers who are super intelligent, able to craft things no one else can," she says looking sideways at me, "There aren't many, but a few."

I'm taken aback enough to freeze. It never occurred to me my intelligence could be a super power. But... no, I shake my head, "I worked for it. I didn't wake up one day and build this suit. I've scraped, clawed, and struggled for every inch. I did the same things every other engineer has done, I just did it four times faster."

Crap, did I give too much away?

"There's a pool you know, in the main clubhouse."

"I don't swim." When you can't kick your legs, water is terrifying. I shudder just thinking about it.

"No, silly," she laughs, "A *betting* pool. On what you are. Care to give me a hint? I'll happily split the winnings with you." I think about it for a minute. I like her, I really do and she seems to like me. I don't want to let any of these people in, but equally, I don't want to learn that she's involved. Can I know for sure? She is only six or seven years older than me which means she couldn't have worked for Cat-7 when it happened. At the same time, she's worked with them since she was eighteen years old.

I inhale sharply and push off from the wall. I take the seat next to her.

"Open faceplate."

The shield slides up revealing my face. I know what she sees, an ordinary girl with brown eyes and the slightly dark skin from her Hispanic mother.

"You're—just a kid?"

"Close faceplate." It slams shut. I don't know why my heart suddenly hurts, but it does. I see her face fall as she realizes. She's an empath after all.

"I'm in my twenties, hardly a child." I slide up and head for the door. This was a mistake. Stupid, stupid, *stupid*.

"Wait, wait. I'm sorry, I just—you weren't what I expected." She's up across the room with a hand on my shoulder. "Please, stay and talk."

I look down at the floor for a moment. My whole life, since the day of the accident, even when I was recovering in the hospital and they told me I would never walk again, I had one goal. One purpose. Find out the truth. My Uncle never believed me and everyone else thought I was delusional, Carlos never really knew me then, being alone is who I am. If I could have my parents back all would be right. In the meantime, it would be nice to have someone else.

But, not today.

"Maybe some other time." As I walk toward the skylight Epic wirelessly signals it to open. I hit the thrusters and in seconds I'm sailing away into the air. Flying always clears my head. With the sun going down I have about two hours of sustained flight time. I angle up and slow down to half speed.

The altimeter rolls past ten thousand feet and I try to switch to hover. It isn't easy.

I let the calm of the air and the quiet of the altitude settle my mind. I am focused. I've worked hard to find the truth. Every piece of evidence has led me to this moment. It also has left me alone. For the first time in years my heart aches for something I haven't ever had. I do need to be careful, but it sure would be nice to have a girl for a friend.

I wish I could trust all of them. The ECM master alarm tells me I can't. They're still trying to track me to my home. Well, time to show them a little something I've been working on.

"Epic, stealth mode."

The HUD changes color from blue to a soft green. The internal lights dim and the sound bafflers kick in. I'm limited to a hundred miles an hour in this mode. I also can't keep it on forever, I have heat collectors obscuring my trail and at some point I need to dump all the heat. The coup de'grace is my kinetic shields. I've tinkered with the frequency, and for a short time, and at a tremendous energy cost, I can project kinetic energy into a wedge which deflects the radar waves around me and not back to the source.

I head home.

The window to my workshop is open when I arrive, a sure sign Carlos has been there. If it were anyone else my security alarms would have triggered an alert. I manage to glide through the window and plant my feet on the floor. The reinforced boards hold. I'm tired, my arms hurt and I'm so ready for bed. The pull bar I have in the center of the room is perfectly angled with the suit's storage vault.

I reach up and grasp the bar. The magnetic field in the vault overrides the suit's and as one piece it flings itself at the wall. My chair drives itself over and I lower myself down. It feels good to sit in the flesh, even if it means I can't walk.

A light breeze blows through my room and clears out some of the hot phoenix air.

"Oh crap," Kate says. I spin around and she's standing three feet from me with a pizza in one hand a six-pack in the other.

"Well, this is a little awkward," she whispers.

ELEVEN

"I'm really sorry," Kate says for the umpteenth time of the evening. I roll over to the window and slide it shut. As soon as it's sealed the AC kicks in and the room drops ten degrees in a few seconds.

"Wow, great AC," she says.

"I pipe it up from the super cooling I use on my computers." I still don't know what to think. I knew she could teleport but I thought she had to be able to see where she was going.

"I just, I didn't know, I thought I would surprise you with pizza and beer as an apology." She holds them up.

"It's okay, really. I didn't want to come clean just yet, but I would have to sooner or later anyways. Are you going to stand there or serve up the pie?" It was odd to see her put out. She was obviously upset. It isn't anything new to me. I don't meet a lot of people because of my obsession with my work. When I do they act awkward and strange because what do you say to the girl who can't walk? 'Hey, sorry you're stuck in a chair'. I often find myself having to get the ball rolling and tonight seemed no different.

I run my hands over my custom wheels and send my chair rolling down the ramp to my living room. The house isn't huge. The kitchen and laundry room are downstairs along with a garage I don't use. Upstairs is my workshop, bedroom, and bathroom. I order in most nights. I rarely even go downstairs except to do laundry. Considering I spend most of my time in my synthsuit and the rest in pajamas or sweats, I don't have a lot of that to do either.

The workshop is slightly higher than my room. It sits on top of the garage. I knocked down the walls of the second floor to make it easier to get around. A ramp leads the way to where I sleep. I also have a couch, a recliner and an even bigger TV than the one Carlos and I play games on. This is my 'movie watching' TV.

I can hear her follow me down. How much should I share with her? Can I trust her? I wish I knew. She sets the pizza down on the low coffee table and takes the chair for herself. I see her mouth open and I hold up my hand.

"If you apologize one more time I'm kicking you out. Kate, I'm in a wheelchair, I'm not dying. Understand?"

She shakes her head and smiles, "Right, of course, I'm acting like an idiot. Here," she opens the pie. Then I notice it's Bianco's.

"It's a Friday night... how did you get this?" Bianco's is like eating perfection. It's my absolute favorite pizza in the whole world and unless I order a week in advance I never eat any. The smell of the pepperoni and cheese fill the room and my mouth instantly waters. Not having eaten all day may have something to do with it.

"I can teleport, I'm a local celebrity, and the night manager is crushing on me hard," she says.

I wolf down a slice for starters then pull myself up and out of my chair to sit on the couch. It's more comfortable and I can spread out a little. I yawn as I talk to her. She holds out a beer to me and I take it without thinking.

"You know I'm only twenty, I can't legally drink this yet," I inform her.

"Okay, I know I came here unannounced—"

"—and uninvited," I add.

"—and uninvited, but girl, you have got to spill. You have a twenty million dollar suit of armor in an attic made of wood. You literally invented something to make you walk, run, fly, and shoot."

"I don't think it's worth twenty-mill—"

"Mayhew put it at twenty-one point four to be exact and he was just talking about the armor. He's frothing at the mouth to find out the process by which you made it. He's convinced it would be worth *hundreds of millions,*" Kate says.

I guess it would be, but I am *never* going to reveal how I do it, not to anyone. I don't have a lot of faith in human nature.

"I guess you're right," I say around a bite, "What's your point?"

"Why are you doing this? Being a super-hero I mean. Surely you could make a fortune as an engineer. You built all of this, you're smart, you could work for anyone." Maybe she can see the hesitance on my face, or maybe it's her empathic abilities. I wish Epic could tell me if she's using her pheromones. I don't feel especially warm toward her, which might mean she's not.

"I make enough for a decent living and more on the side for the extra stuff, but this..."

"How many degrees do you have?" I ask her.

"Me? One, a bachelor's in marketing. My powers developed before they had the test to detect them. I was a few months out of college when I found out, you?"

"None."

I don't think this woman is stunned often, and here I've done it twice in one night. I can't help but smile. Another slice of pizza is on deck but by the time I'm done with half of it I can't eat anymore. I love it, but a slice and a half is my limit.

"You have to have something?"

"The great thing about being disabled, besides parking, are all the school programs people will let you do from home. Being a tad anti-social, I applied for all of them. I just wanted to read the books. I read them, learned them, and moved on."

"When did you finish?"

"Learning or reading?" I ask.

"Is there a difference?" she replies.

"I stopped reading the college books when I was eleven. At fourteen I was writing papers under a pseudonym, at sixteen I sold a piece of tech to Lockheed-Martin that will soon be in every airplane for the next hundred years. I finished the suit last year, but I've been working on it since I was seven years old."

I'm enjoying the shocked look on her face entirely too much. I don't tell this story often, and it's always fun to let people know exactly how smart I am. Not in a patronizing 'I'm better than you' way, but in the, 'this is who I am'. A moment of regret washes over me. I have sacrificed everything for this. What if they're gone? No, I can't think like that. *I saw what I saw.*

"If you had degrees, how many would you have?" she asks.

"It's hard to say, four, maybe five if you count chemistry."

"Four bachelors? I could hardly stand one."

I cough out beer through my nose. I grab a napkin and wipe my face. It burns my nose, but the taste is pleasant enough.

"Doctorates, Kate. Metallurgy, physics, quantum mechanics, Engineering, and chemistry. Plus a handful of other lesser degrees. I spend a lot of time reading."

I nibble at my last slice as I wait for her to absorb it all. I glance over at the monitor above the suit to see the recharge progress and if Epic needs any help with the firmware update. I sketched out a program for him to allow me better access in the future if for some reason he can't assist me.

"Oh, I forgot Computer Science. Whoops. So six." I say.

"Okay, I'm officially impressed. You did all this and you have no superpowers?"

I shake my head, "Nada."

"Have you had the test?"

"I don't need it, I'm telling you Kate, I don't have them. I'm just dedicated, and driven."

"No one's this driven." She's finally starting to relax. It feels good to open up to someone. I make the call. If I tell her now, on my terms, then I can control how things go from here.

"I can tell you want to say something, what?"

"When I was six years old my family was on a trip to southern California. I don't remember a whole lot about it. My dad loved road trips. He said it calmed him. Him and mom would talk for hours. In this instance I was falling asleep off and on. I think we were on our way to San Diego. The plan was to go to Sea World."

I stop to take a pull from the beer. Everyone else I have ever told the whole story to has thought I was delusional at best, a liar at worst.

"You can trust me, Amelia, I promise," she says. Her green eyes bore into mine and I believe her. I nod,

"My mom screamed suddenly and we plunged off a cliff." I close my eyes, the memories I keep hidden boiling to the surface.

"The car rolled. I was flung against my seatbelt then the door came off and back in and crushed me against the seat. I don't know what happened next, but I woke up and I was upside down. I was crying and calling for my dad. He was there, Kate. He was holding my hand and telling me it would be okay. I could hear mom, too, she was on the phone." The next part was the worst and I desperately didn't want to cry. The tears clouded my eyes and I squeezed them shut.

"I opened my eyes again and they were gone. No bodies, nothing. The next time I woke up I was in the hospital. I couldn't move my legs and everyone was telling me my parents were dead. They weren't, I saw them, I know they weren't."

Silence fills the room as I finish. I take another drink and rub my eyes with my sleeve.

"What happened?" she asks.

"That is the million-dollar question, isn't it. My dad worked for Cat-7 and I swear that is who my mom was talking to when I heard her on the phone. Everyone told me I had imagined it, that I'd made it up to avoid seeing their dead bodies in the front seat. I don't know, maybe I did, but I don't think so."

She puts her beer down and leans forward, cocking her head to the side as she examines me.

"You're not lying. Even if you were lying to yourself, even if you had made up the whole thing, a part of you would know the truth. You can't hide the truth from an empath."

A wave of euphoria rolls over me. My whole life I'd carried the burden of not knowing. Had I lied to myself? Now I know. I almost cry.

"Thank you, god, thank you."

"Now the question is, what are you going to do about it?" she asks.

TWELVE

It's almost normal, flying around Phoenix in a lazy arc as the sun shines down on me. The baffles in my armor keep the majority of the sound out as the wind buffets me and the jets roar. I have to say, I love this city. The food, the entertainment, everything. Especially the food.

A burden has lifted from my shoulders, I don't know how telling Kate about what happened made me feel so much better, but it did. Maybe with a little help, I can move this much faster. Infiltrate Cat-7 and find out where my parents are and why Cat-7 took them. *Are they still alive?*

No, I can't afford to think that way. There would be no reason to kidnap them if they were just going to let them die. After all, they could have just left them to die in the car. They went to a lot of trouble to take them and not let anyone know. They had to still be alive.

"Arsenal, this is central, there is a report of a superhuman sighting in Tucson. How quickly can you be there?" Epic hears everything I hear and before I can even consider it he flashes the time up on my HUD.

"About thirty minutes, you want me to go?"

"Affirmative. The computer says likely targets are a group of banks around Arizona national."

Epic threw up the map of Tucson for me. Yeah, four banks all within a few blocks of each other. Brilliant.

"Roger, I'll head there now. Can you notify the team in case I need backup?"

"Will do, Central out."

I didn't recognize the voice on the other end, but that wasn't anything new. They must have a huge rotation of people to be the communications HUB for all the state teams. Still, I preferred it when I received my instructions from our own people.

"Epic, let's lock up the suit and set a ballistic trajectory. I don't want to be exhausted when we arrive." He does all the math for me. I pull up until the lines on my HUD are in sync and then the suit goes rigid. The thrusters roar and I am up in the sky.

I pick up a tail wind on the way down and shave seven minutes off my time. I see Tucson up ahead. Funny, I've lived in Arizona for almost fifteen years and I don't think I've ever left Phoenix. Tucson isn't as big as Phoenix, but it is still a big city. We hit five thousand feet and Epic unlocks me. I take manual control and curl us around to the north.

"Go full active on the sensors, also tap the local news, Youtube, etc."

I have done this before.

"Yeah, yeah," I mutter. I come in a low arc over the banking complex. People on the ground are waving up at me, snapping pictures. They probably don't know who I am. Flying heroes are still cool to see. I would wave back but I can't without changing my flight path.

The white van parked in down the street has a high level of thermal radiation. Not dangerous, but extremely unusual.

"Well, let's check it out, shall we?"

They're parked near the intersection, giving them easy access to three places with high-value cash grabs. This doesn't feel right. I slide down to a hundred feet above the middle of the street. I'm not trying to come right at them, but if I can fly close enough maybe Epic can better scan it.

"Epic, put me through to the HQ, I think I want backup."

My HUD blinks, as if I changed the channel on the TV, it shouldn't do that.

We're being—

He doesn't have time to finish. The van's back doors fly open and three men in tactical gear with hi-tech looking rifles leap out. The rifles are the source of the heat. They all take a knee as one and open fire on me.

"Whoa," I shout. I spin the armor as green bolts of something hot blows by me.

Experimental plasma rifles. Threat level unknown.

I pull a spin to follow their trajectory. They splash into the building behind me and explode inward. Facade and glass shower the streets. Okay, don't be hit by them. I throw my hands out to halt my forward momentum and crash to the ground twenty feet from them. They're aiming again. I lunge to the side and the bolts catch a mid-sized sedan behind me. Flames engulf the suit as the car explodes. This is going from bad to worse.

"Epic, I need backup, now!"

It will take me a moment to send a message via the Internet. If he has to use the internet the radio is being jammed, awesome. I let off a blast with my IP cannons in their general direction. The van's windshield shatters but I miss them. Thrusters on. A bolt of green passes through where I was. I hear the explosion behind me. Okay, kid gloves off, before someone gets killed.

"Pod them as I fly by."

It's bad luck one of the men shoots as soon as I launch the pod, it's vaporized in super heated fire. I'm close to them now, IP cannons blast out again. The blue ionic energy washes over them... then dissipates into the ground with no effect. That isn't possible. There is no frigging way they have armor specially designed to resist my weapons.

"Any luck?"

Domino is in a meeting with the governor, her cell phone is off. Major Force and Mr. Perfect are in the Portland base, but they have no way of arriving here in time to affect the outcome.

I want to curse so bad right now. I kick in the jets full power and pull up. Trails of green energy follow me. They weren't ready for my speed burst. I shoot high up, about a thousand feet then pull over and loop back down. By the time I'm level with the pavement, I'm four hundred feet away from them, two feet above the ground, flying at a hundred miles an hour.

"Lock me up!" I shout, barely in time as I cover the distance in four seconds. I hit all three, plow into the van and explode out the other side. A large pickup truck stops my charge. The metal of the bed crumples around me.

It takes me a second to free myself. One of the men is embedded in the truck with me, I don't think he's getting back up. Another is moaning on the street fifty feet away. I don't see the third—the whine of his plasma rifle charging registers. Epic fires my grenade launcher, the pod hits his rifle and pulls his aim off. The green bolt hits the ruined truck behind me.

My ramming speed maneuver charged my kinetic lance, I bracket him and fire as he struggles to put his barrel back on target. The beam of force hits him square in the chest and sends him flying into the brick building behind him. He slides to the ground, down, but not dead. Epic's sensors tell me the grisly news. The other two are dead.

"Show me the source of the jamming."

An arrow pops up on my HUD and I follow it to the back of the van. My mad flight ripped the roof off, but the stuff on the inside is still there. I hold out my hand and fire a pulse into it. Sparks fly and suddenly I can hear again.

"Central, I need the police and EMS to my location."

No response.

"This is Arsenal calling the Diamondbacks dispatcher, come in?"

Still nothing, fine.

"Put me through to the local PD, Epic, I'll just call it in myself."

THIRTEEN

It's been two hours since it happened. Epic finally found a way to message Domino and she should be here any second. The problem I have right now is that Central is claiming they didn't send me down here. When I tried to call them earlier and no one answered, it was because our local monitors were supposed to be on duty. Except, they had been called to Portland HQ and assured Central was online. Central wasn't monitoring me because they were assured my local team had me.

I smell a setup. Plasma weapons? Who even has those. Epic pulls up a virtual diagram for me of the weapons. I've spent the last two hours going through them, their tech is way past possible into the realm of impossible. Of course, I'm sitting in a suit that isn't possible, I'm not exactly one to complain. Still, they couldn't have been here to rob anything. Those guns are worth millions on the black market.

I hear a pop, thank god.

"Arsenal, what happened?" Ugh, not the voice I wanted to hear. Luke walks toward me, his face tells me he isn't happy, but at least he's not yelling at me.

"You could read the police report, or the one I filed after the jamming ended, or watch my in-suit camera." I amped up my camera to include full video and sound after the *Deadman* incident. I don't want to be framed for something. I know this is the wrong thing to say when the vein above his eye twitches.

"Well then, let me tell you what I know. You came down here without being asked and shot up a street, destroyed private property, and killed two men, sound about right?"

I catch a glimpse of Domino speaking to the local cops, I'm glad she's here, she can put the rage man back in his box if needed. Except, she's over there and he's right here in front of me. He certainly loses all his appeal when he's mad. I can't say I blame him about being mad. I take a deep breath and try not to sound snarky.

"Everything but the part about being asked."

"Who asked you?"

"Central, they called me—" He waves his hand at me to interrupt. I have to clench my jaw to keep from biting his head off.

"Central has no record of sending you here, in fact they have multiple attempts at calling you to explain yourself which you ignored."

No wonder he's mad. At least he isn't yelling at me. This was a setup. Dammit. I knew the risks when I joined, in a way this is good. It confirms what I already knew. Cat-7 was behind my parents disappearance, and now they want me out of the picture.

"I can give you the recordings on my end, they called me. I don't know what's going on here, Major, but I didn't do anything wrong."

"Tell that to the two dead guys over there." He turns and walks away before I can respond.

"Jerk," I say inside my helmet. My gut hurts and I suddenly very much want the faceplate off. I don't care the circumstances, or how much they brought it on themselves, I killed two men.

I'm detecting elevated cardiac vitals. I recommend deep calming breathes.

"Thanks. Domino, I need you..."

"One sec, just clearing things up with—"

"Now, please."

She's beside me in a second. Another second later we're in my home. Her teleportation is vastly different than the quantum elevator. I don't feel anything, I blink and I'm home. I lurch over to the bar and grab the handles. The suit flies off of me in a hurry and my chair slides underneath me. The bar lowers me down into the seat.

I put my head down as low as I can and try to take deep calming breaths.

"Amelia... are you okay?"

"I could use some of those calming pheromones of yours right about now."

She kneels down beside me, a hand on my shoulder speaks soothing words to me.

"It'll be okay. I know it isn't easy, when this happens, but it's part of the job."

I know she's using her powers on me, the logic of that doesn't keep it from working. My chest loosens up and I feel like I can breathe again.

"It was a setup, Kate, plain and simple."

She shakes her head, "They're part of a hi-tech cabal. They've hit three or four central banks in the last six months using experimental weapons and communications tech. No one knows where they get it, or how. For that matter, why they use it to rob banks. They've gotten away with almost a hundred million dollars. It wasn't a setup, it was bad luck."

I shake my head and run my hands through my hair. No, it was. I wheel over to my mini-fridge and pop a Coke. I offer one to her, which she takes. I open mine and drink. Even with Kate's whammy, I'm in shock, I know I am. Sugar helps, intellectually I know this, but it takes a few moments to remove the edge.

"Then why doesn't *Central* have a record of sending me there?"

She sips her soda for a few seconds before replying, "Okay, you may have a point, but it could have been a technical glitch."

"I'm not prepared to go full *coast to coast* just yet, but something is fishy."

"Come back to HQ when you're feeling better, we still have to file official reports and what not. Don't be too long and," she puts her hand on my shoulder and I can smell her perfume, which means her pheromones are working on me and my head clears a little, "don't be too quick, either."

FOURTEEN

I'm flying through the air on my way to Las Vegas when it hits me. I need to super cool the quantum field while heating the core! It's so simple I almost missed it. The only question is, can I adapt it to Arsenal? If I can, even in a limited capacity, I can amp up almost every aspect of the suit. I grin at the possibilities

"—Do you copy, Arsenal?" Major Force asks.

Crap, I was too busy daydreaming to hear him.

"Negative, sir, uh it's noisy out here." I can hear him sigh in over the comlink. I'm still on probation and I haven't impressed too many people. Deadman died, and there was a lot of suspicion on me. Luckily, a nearby surveillance camera cleared me. Beyond him, there hasn't been a lot of opportunity to prove myself. There was the bank robbery which couldn't have gone worse if I tried. Then the PR stunt Kate put together to save the cat from the tree. I almost died laughing on the job. She says with how absolutely bad ass my red and white armor looks, I could easily be the next big thing on the toy circuit.

"The Las Vegas PD reports sightings of at least three F3's in the city. Superpowers of any kind are banned in the city, which is what triggered the alert. They're there to rob a casino, or pull some other sort of job. We need to locate them and bring them in with as little property damage as possible. Understood?"

There is a chorus of 'yes' and 'roger' over the net. "Understood," I say. Mostly to be different.

"Do we know who?" I ask.

"Jack Danger is the only one we know of for sure. The other two set off the alarms when they attempted to enter the MGM grand." Meta-human sniffers developed by none other than Category-7 work by detecting a hundred different biometric readings from a person. In a microsecond they correlate them to all known metas and then make a best guess. It works surprisingly well. The more they detect, the more accurate they become. It turns out, almost every meta has altered brain waves or metabolic processes. It only takes one for the sniffer to work.

"If you check your staff email you will see the portfolio central has sent over on JD. Remember, he's strong, fast, and agile. On top of everything else he can do, don't underestimate him. If he's here with two others, then he's in charge. Questions?"

No one asks any, so I don't.

"We're twenty minutes out, read the file and be ready."

The transport we're flying on is a private Gulfstream modified for in-flight departure. Since my armor works best in sunlight I opted to use the rigging on the belly to fly instead of being inside. It isn't like I would pop my mask for a drink. I run a detailed note past Epic on my thoughts on Zero Point energy, then I dive into the email.

Danger really is dangerous. He's capable of deadlifting three tons, he can run at seventy miles an hour. Jump a half mile from a dead stop and has low-level invulnerability. Nothing short of a sniper rifle can penetrate his skin and he's been hit by a mac truck and walked away. On top of all of his other abilities he can emit a low-level EMP with a touch of his fingers. He's been known to induce heart attacks and shut down buildings. Lucky for me, he can't touch my skin and the armor is of course shielded from EMP. It would be pretty stupid to be flying around in armor which could be shut off by a strong solar flare.

"Arsenal, we're going to do a flyby of the city, I want you to detach and find us a roof top on the strip near the grand."

"Roger," I reply immediately. It wouldn't do for him to not like me. As irritating as he is, he's the final say on if I'm let on the team. Kate has assured me no one goes more than a month on probation. A month passed by yesterday.

The jet circles the city once. As it lines up for the airport they slow the engines to allow me to detach. I pull the harness and I'm falling. I've never been skydiving before, I've watched a lot of videos on it, but never done it. This would have to be as close as I get. I pin my arms and legs straight like an arrow and ignite my thrusters. They roar to life. I hit my top speed in a few seconds.

"Epic, full sensor sweep. Access the local cameras if you can and give us a bit more spread." The team could have access to the cameras in retrospect, but with Epic we can have him monitoring them live.

On it.

I put my hands in front of me to slow my thrust and bring my suit up to hover over the Hard Rock cafe, it looks like the only place with a roof flat enough to stand on. Sadly, it isn't very high.

After I land I lean over the edge and scan the crowd, I'm not really looking, just giving Epic a chance to 'see' everything.

"You in position, Arsenal?"

"Yep."

I hear a pop behind me, followed by a second one. Force leans out over the edge next to me. "You couldn't have found a taller building?"

I restrain my biting response about his observation skills. "This is the only one with a flat surface."

"It will have to do." He holds his hand up to his ear to speak to central.

"ETA on the containment team?"

I don't hear the response because I'm not tuned to the frequency, but from the look on his face I can tell he's not happy.

"And if we can't?"

I'm tempted to eavesdrop. However there are more pressing things happening. I want Epic's full computing cycles on finding JD. Two more rapid pops behind me and we have the full team. Force, Domino, Mr. Perfect, and me. We're not exactly heavy hitters. If JD's compatriots have any non-punchy powers, we could be in trouble. I go over my load out. I put the pods after my bean bag rounds. I don't know how effective they would be against a guy who can short things out. Four bean bags, four pods. Worse case I can hit his men with them. Kinetic lance is on, but it won't charge until I'm hit. IP Cannons are ready to go, their capacitors are fully charged. The first shot will be full power. Finally, I bring the particle beam on-line. I can only power it minimally without severely affecting the other systems. My capacitors are at full and all the power I can produce is accounted for.

Mr. Perfect strides over to the side to look down at the strip. His costume, or uniform, or whatever, is a bright red suit with a black tie, he carries a magician's cane in one hand and his other is gloved. He also wears a Phantom of the Opera mask. I don't know why, his identity is public. Major Force has a military cut jacket, cargo pants and boots. He looks like he's still an active duty Marine. His concession to the team is his mask, it covers his forehead and eyes down to his cheeks. It's black and dangerous looking.

Domino is the most stylish, but I would expect her to be. She wears a black form fitting catsuit with several belts, buckles and pockets. She carries a lot of small gear with her, two pistols, Tasers, and even a grenade for if things go badly. Her ability to teleport is a tactical asset not to be underestimated.

Epic is bracketing everyone on the strip, running facial recognition in the blink of an eye. If they're out there, he will find them.

"Do we know of any possible targets?" asks Domino.

"The local PD says there are two fights tonight with large purses, not to mention the casinos are packed for the long weekend," Force replies.

For some reason I thought we would land and the bad guys would come running out of cover and we would fight. I'm not a police officer, I don't know how to investigate things, and I certainly can't go around asking people *have you seen this man*?

"Out of curiosity," I say with my synthesized voice, "Why are we here?"

Force grunts at me. "Weren't you listening to my briefing?"

"Yeah, I heard your briefing, and I read the file."

"Then you know why we're here." He says as if it is obvious.

Domino glances at me and raises an eyebrow. Her eyes shine like jewels in the night and I wonder for a second if it is part of her empathic powers. I shake my head to focus.

"No, I know why *a* team was sent, what I'm asking is why this team was sent?"

"If you're not up for a little danger, proby," Mr. Perfect chimes in, "you're in the wrong line of business."

"None of you think it's odd we were sent? Jack Danger is on the FBI's top ten powers wanted list. He's rated an F3, and he has two F3's with him. I don't know what you all have rated me as, but it is probably F2—"

"That's for damn sure," Major Force says with a snarl. To his credit he hasn't taken his eyes off the street.

"So, I ask again, why this team? We're shorthanded and doing the math I'm not sure we're capable of taking on three F3's."

Domino puts her hand to her earpiece, "Sighting, two blocks North. They're out in the open. The sniffers picked them up as the passed the north entrance."

Force smiles as he turns to face us, "We're here because it is our job and we're paid to protect people. If you don't like it," he points his big finger at me, "you can walk whenever you want."

I clench my jaw trying not to say anything but this is too much.

"Dude, what is your problem? Is it because I'm a woman, or because I don't have any powers? You've been an asshole to me since the day we met."

His eyes widen and the little vein above his eye twitches.

"Force, Arsenal, now is not the time," Domino breaks in, stepping between us, "Focus on the mission."

Mission, right. I don't know how these people don't see this, it feels like a setup to me.

"We'll talk about this after, Arsenal. Right now I need you to fly recon. Perfect, go on the ground, blend in and be ready to strike. Domino," he turns to her, "'Port us there now."

I look at her as she moves beside him. She puts her hand on his shoulder. I'm tempted to open my faceplate and tell her to be safe. Instead I nod. I hear a pop and they're gone.

"Epic, stealth mode and blast off."

FIFTEEN

The strip from two-hundred feet is beautiful. Neon lights reflect off of everything casting brilliant hues and shadows. It's also playing havoc with thermal imaging. I switch to enhanced and I'm looking at the street as if I were fifty feet above instead of two-hundred.

"I've got them," Perfect says over the comms. His voice sounds cocky and arrogant. I know it's part of his persona but I want to punch him in the face.

"Epic, if I go unconscious for any reason, activate safety protocols. I can't have people trying to remove the armor from me."

Affirmative.

I zoom to where Perfect is. He's changed his appearance somehow, he has a tux on and a gorgeous blonde in an evening dress to hang on his arm. The only reason I know it's him is his comm pings my HUD. I knew he could make constructs... but holograms?

"Be ready, they're coming up on our position."

I track forward until I find them. Three men, walking afield of each other. They have a confident stride about them. The one in the middle is Danger, his ID pops up on my screen. Epic flags the one to his right—Foehunter. What kind of stupid name is—crap, he's bad ass. Low-level speedster with hands like razors. Apparently he's a world class martial artist and can cut people to ribbons in a few seconds.

Epic flashes me a warning. The third guy has no ID.

"Force, the one on the right is Foehunter, the guy on the left is unknown." I tell him over the comms.

"What? How do you know? Central doesn't have an ID on anyone but Danger."

"I'm telling you, it's Foehunter, keep Domino back, this guy will chew up anyone who isn't armored or invulnerable." There is a moment of silence. He can't seriously dislike me enough to risk her life?

"Kate, what do you think?"

"You may not like her, but if Arsenal says it's him, it's him." I smile. I feel my cheeks warm in the armor and I try not to cough from embarrassment. I don't think anyone has ever expressed faith in me to such a degree.

"Alright, hang back," Force says, "Perfect, you've dealt with the guy, is it him?" asks Force. While they talk Epic locks on to each of them. I could spray bean bags at them and follow up with AG pods. It might catch them by surprise.

"I'm close enough give me a—yeah, that's his ugly ass. If I can get closer I can wrap him up easy enough."

I'm tempted to have Epic shunt power to my cannons and open with a barrage of ionic pulses. However, I would have to drop stealth to do it and I don't think—

The trio stops. In a very familiar gesture, Jack raises his hand to his ear. They have overwatch? This feels less and less like some robbery and more like an orchestrated plan.

"I think they've made—" I don't get to finish. Foehunter vanishes in a blur of speed. He moves through the crowd and in a blink slashes Mr. Perfect from chin to thigh. Mr. Perfect flies back against the fountain he was standing at and falls in the water. A dark stain spreads out from where he's laying, his tux vanishes along with the girl who had been hanging on his arm.

"Pierre!" Domino screams over the comms.

Force roars as he barrels in. It wasn't my imagination, the guy gets frigging huge when he powers up. Three or four inches taller, at least six wider. He runs straight at Jack Danger.

"Domino, I'll tag Foehunter, get Mr. Perfect to a hospital!"

"Ready," she says.

"Epic, drop stealth, charge cannons."

Suddenly, heat bleeds from my suit and the air around me lights up as my thrusters go full power. I fling my arms behind me to dive down. When I'm forty feet away, Foehunter turns to face me. For some reason he isn't leaving Perfect, it's like he knows someone will try to rescue him. It's then I notice his collateral damage. As he moved through the crowd he cut everyone he passed. Some minor, some severe. A trail of blood follows him spattered across the concrete.

"Domino, do you see it?" I ask as I throw my arms up to halt my forward momentum and flip up to land. I've seen footage of me landing, I know how impressive the suit looks. I don't bother with witty banter, I aim my left hand at him and fire. The pulse cannon's energy is on a narrow beam, only five inches wide. I have a perfect lock on—he's gone. The cannon impacts the fountain and channels into the ground. My kinetic shield drops ten percent... twenty... thirty... he's hitting me with lightning fast strikes, each blow coming in faster than I can make out.

Three more strikes and I'm down to twenty percent shielding. The lance is fully charged though. I smile, "Epic, drop kinetic shielding."

The field fades around me. I feel the next blow land. It hits my shoulder and spins me around. I also hear him scream in pain. He's standing ten feet away from me, holding his hand as it drips blood on the ground.

"You seem to have some performance issues. Maybe you should see a shrink," my synthesized voice says. I'm sure the sarcasm came across when his face turns into a mask of rage. He blurs and his foot hits me in the face knocking me back. I guess he's not going to try and cut me. Epic signals Domino's departure as she teleports Mr. Perfect away. He's annoying, but I hope he makes it.

How do they do it without armor? I don't have time to ponder it now. Foehunter is throwing every object he can find at me. It results in a small meteor shower of rocks, tire irons, lug nuts and anything else he can find to hurl.

"Epic, is there any pattern?"

He's chaotic. If you could stop him for one second I could fire the lance and bring him down.

"Good plan, but how do I stop him?"

I check on Force. He and Jack Danger are dancing around each other, both are incredibly skilled in hand-to-hand. Except when they miss, parts of the landscape are destroyed. While I'm watching, Force dodges a kick and the side of a very expensive car caves in from the blow. Force comes up and knocks Danger to the ground. It dissolves into a ground game and I can't spare any more time for it. At least I know he's okay.

"You know what, *Foehunter,*" I put a lot of emphasis on his name, "You win. Go ahead and run away, I have more important things to do."

He appears in front of me, a spear from what must be a Chinese prop pointed at me. His mouth opens to retort and Epic fires.

The lance catches him as he blurs away. Instead of a smooth line to his destination, he runs headfirst into a concrete wall. I'm not sure the level of his invulnerability, but the way he falls flat back tells me he's out.

"Fire all bean bags at him."

The *puff* of compressed air makes me smile as his body twitches from the impact. Once they're depleted I pod him. When I turn away his form is slowly rising into the air.

Force and Danger are a blur of motion, punching and kicking each other. I'm not sure they could hurt me, but my armor only slightly enhances my strength. I should look into fixing that. Right now there is one more guy—there he is. Sitting on the steps to the casino, eating an apple?

"Epic, scan him please."

My entire sensor suite comes online. It draws significant power and the lights inside the suit dim. I would have preferred doing this during the day as I have no way to recharge without a hookup or solar power. I smile inwardly, of course now that I understand the Zero-Point Field, I should be able to do something about it.

"Arsenal, stop standing there and help me!" Force yells from behind. I'm not sure what he wants me to do. I turn and bracket Danger. He's got Force down on one knee and is repeatedly bashing him in the face.

"Epic, pod him." The *puff* of air signals launch. Danger jerks back in surprise. I guess he expected it to explode or something. When he's twenty feet in the air he starts laughing.

Force looks at me incredulously.

I shrug, "Unless you're telling me to kill him, it's all I got."

Force snarls. He's breathing heavy and I know he's at his limit.

"How long?"

"Until I shut it off."

He takes a few steps toward Danger.

Alarm bells ring on my screen. Epic flashes a radiation warning and all my passive sensors are going haywire.

"Epic?"

The unknown man with the apple is building up to some sort of explosion. Based on the thermal energy and the gamma rays his body is giving off, he's going nuclear, possibly a one-kiloton yield.

Epic throws up a countdown. We don't have much time. I fire a pod at the living bomb. Epic reads his body temp at four hundred degrees. The pod hits him in the chest and activates. I'm not sure how long the pod will last, I didn't design them to withstand thermal distress. I don't need it to last long. I hit my thrusters full and slam into him. I put one hand on his belt and the other I use to maneuver. It isn't the easiest and my left arm feels like it's going to rip out of its socket.

We're pointed up and everything is full power. My radio kicks on and I can hear Force trying to talk to me. The radiation from apple boy is too much and the signal can't get through.

My HUD shuts off and I can't access any of my controls, however I'm pointed up and the suit is still blasting away. I don't think we're high enough, and if he detonates... a nuclear bomb burns five times as hot as the sun. Titanium-Tungsten Carbide armor will be as useful as a piece of tissue against a nuclear fire. I glance down. It's been at least thirty seconds—at two hundred mph it is a mile and a half easy. I can feel the heat in my hand. I'm amazed my pod is still working at this point.

"Epic," I scream. Just a few more seconds and I can let him go. Ten...nine...eight...my hand feels like I've stuck it in a fire. I need to reach two miles. He's glowing now, I close my eyes but it doesn't do any good.

This is all I have, I hope it's enough. I let him go. My thrusters quit out and I'm falling. I watch as he continues to float up. I've got to be at terminal velocity. He's just a spec now and—A light flares to life so bright it is like looking at the sun.

My faceplate goes black to protect my vision—

SIXTEEN

Science has solved every problem I've ever had in my life. Usually the science of blowing things up, but science all the same.
    -From the journal of Amelia Lockheart

The first thing I hear is the soft beeps and hums of heart monitors and breathing machines. Oh god, did they peel me out of the armor? I struggle to open my eyes, it's like they're wrapped in gauze, but finally I see some light. Everything is blurry. I can smell antiseptic air, but I don't feel the suit on me.

"She's awake," I hear a man's voice I don't recognize.

I try to ask for water but it comes out as a mumble. Something cool and wet is pushed to my lips and I sip it up. My throat is raw, it hurts to swallow.

"Where—" I manage to spit out. Everything is floaty and indistinct. I must be on loads of painkillers. *If they took me out of the suit how come I'm not dead?*

"I'll go get your friends." The male voice says. "You can come in now, both of you." My vision is still not a hundred percent. Two indistinct blobs, one with shoulder-length blonde hair, and one with a crew cut. Great, he's here to yell at me.

I try to raise my hand, instead it just shakes a little.

"Ms. Lockheart, try not to move dear. You've suffered a major concussion, contusions across half your body and somehow managed to get second-degree burns on your hands and face. You're lucky to be alive. Honestly, a person in your situation shouldn't be skydiving."

I can see now, the doc is an older fellow, the grandfatherly sort. Next to him are Kate, and Major Force, Luke. Even in civilian clothes he still screams *marine*.

"Skydiving?" I mutter.

"Yes, don't you remember? We told you it was a bad idea but you insisted," Kate says.

I'm really confused. I look back and forth between them and then to the doc, "I promise I will never jump out of an airplane again."

"Good, because I don't think you could survive a second fall from such a height. It's a miracle you survived this one." He shakes his head as he walks toward the exit.

After he leaves the room I point at the water. Kate moves to grab it but Luke intercepts her and picks it up. He carefully moves it to my lips. I swallow a little more but most of it dribbles down my chin.

He dabs at it with a cloth. "For what it's worth, I was wrong," he looks at Kate, "and a jackass, I'm sorry."

"How?" I manage to say. My throat is feeling better by the second and the fuzz is clearing from my mind.

"When we couldn't find you after the blast we figured you were either vaporized or in the desert somewhere," Kate said. "You forget I can... *boop,*" she makes a funny sound while wiggling her fingers, "to anyone I know—uh, well. Imagine my surprise when I appeared in your workshop. Your AI—Epic? Cool name by the way, he helped me get you out of the suit. After we got you free it was easy enough to bring you here. This is Maricopa county hospital, not affiliated with the Diamondbacks in any way."

I nod, "What happened after?" I seem to be able to use a few more words each time.

"He was three miles up when he detonated. We got a sun tan, all the power went out, and not much else. It would have been horrific if he had detonated at ground level. You saved a couple of million people, Amelia."

I shrug trying to ignore the staggering number of people.

"And Perfect?"

Kate smiled, "He's fine. He'd fought the douchebag before and had his armor spell on. It was more of a bleeding cut than a damaging one."

Despite how annoying he is, I find myself glad he survived. However, I must have serious head trauma, Major Force spoke civilly to me and he used my real name.

"I take it the cat is out of the bag then?" I ask.

He gave me an odd look.

"On my name." I clarify.

"Oh, yes. Also, Kate?" he asks.

She smiles lifting up a briefcase and opening it. Inside is a shiny medal, along with an ID. They used my state ID picture, not the best one I've ever taken. Kate pushes down on the pic and it morphs into Arsenal. The information changed as well.

"Welcome to the Diamondbacks," she says with a smile.

If I grinned any broader they would need a surgeon in here.

"Guys, this is great. Really. However, can you call the doctor back in here?"

They both looked alarmed.

"What's wrong?" asks Luke as he moves to the door.

"I can't feel my legs..."

It took a second but they got it. The three of us burst out laughing at the same time.

"Something is seriously wrong with you," Kate says between breaths.

SEVENTEEN

It turns out, when you're a superhero, a genius, and you wear a suit of armor to fight crime, your team doesn't really like it if your armor is stored in your suburban house. I tried to explain to them the necessity of me living wherever my armor is. Kate's solution? Well, since I was wholeheartedly against moving into the shared HQ underneath Portland, she decided to remodel the two empty offices into one large workshop/living space.

"I don't know about this," I say as I wheel myself off the elevator.

"It's going to be great," the gorgeous blonde walking next to me says.

"Kate, you have to understand how hard it is for me to live someplace... not mine. What about Carlos? How is he supposed to come visit me? What about security? You guys have a direct pipeline to Mr. Personality and I'm pretty sure he tried to kill me and steal my armor."

She shakes her head, "Carlos can take a bus to get here, we're only thirty minutes away. I even gave him a special badge. He was thrilled," she says with a smile. I'll bet he was thrilled. Kate's the kind of woman men fawn over. Even if she wasn't a low-level empath with pheromone projection, she's still a leggy blonde with a figure most women would kill for. Most, not me. I have my own priorities and romance isn't on the list.

"As for the other matter, we have our own security—something I expect you will be upgrading."

"Obviously."

"I don't know why they're doing what they're doing, Amelia, but we're a team, we'll help. Cat-7 may control a lot of what we do and have, but we answer to the Governor and the State. Maybe if this were a national team and was more about politics it would be different, but it isn't. We have your back."

"Thanks, Kate, it means a lot to me."

We pass by Luke's office and I can't help but look in. The room is as spartan as I would imagine, he glances at me as we pass. He smiles and my thoughts of *no* romance vanish. Luke Lancaster, aka Major Force. Ex-Marine, team leader and a hard ass. At least until I saved Las Vegas. Of course, maybe it's because he found out I'm in a wheelchair, I'm not sure which. I do know my stomach does funny things when I catch a glimpse of his crystal blue eyes, or the way his mouth crinkles up when he smiles. His abs of steel and chiseled arms don't hurt. I shake my head, no, no, no. I don't know if I can trust any of them. I want to, but can I? Kate is easy, but the rest... if they're ordered to take me down, would they?

Kate walks into the room in front of me. The techs I hired have done a bang up job of moving my personal workshop here. Arsenal is suspended in its electromagnetic field, waiting to go into action. There's a pull bar in front so I can reach up and stand while the armor wraps around me. I've got my super computer with liquid cooling behind the holding area. I didn't tell them why I needed my computer specifically. Luke and Kate know about Epic, but no one else needs to know. He's been my best friend since the day I turned him on. It took years to make him work. Up until now, all I've had is him and Carlos. Now there's Kate to add to the mix.

The living quarters look exactly like mine did at home. There are a few subtle improvements, but for the most part all the same.

"This had to cost an arm and a leg," I say as I spin my chair three-sixty to look around.

"Yes, but you're worth it." She walks over to the TV and flips it on. She glances to make sure the door is shut before she speaks, "Epic, show her."

"Wait, what? Are you colluding with *my* AI to keep secrets from me?"

"Not, exactly," she replies as the TV fills with footage. It's the fight in Las Vegas. It's split screen and there are several different camera angles. Some look professional, others like cell phone footage.

"On any given day," a voice in the background says, "there are twenty-five superhuman events in the United States." I realize the voice belongs to the broadcaster, the one who does the show on Sundays, but I can't remember his name.

"Superhumans who break the law, who use their miraculous gifts for petty, selfish reasons, are often labeled *supervillains*. A child's name for a very, very dangerous breed of criminal. Perhaps criminal is no longer the right word." The audio from the cameras picks up. There's scuffling and screaming. I can hear Luke and Danger fighting it out and he screams at me for help. I turn, and I look so much more *casual* than I felt. My grenade launcher flips over my shoulder and fires. Danger lifts off and starts his maniacal laugh.

"He's in the supermax, right?" I ask in a whisper. Kate nods, "shh, this is the best part."

I lived it, I'm not sure I would call this the best part.

"Oh my god," someone screams, "he's going to explode!"

I didn't realize he was already glowing when I hit him. I can see the pod smack him and then I'm on him. My thrusters roar as I drive him up into the atmosphere. All the cameras drop away but one. Someone must have had a super-telephoto lens to track me.

"There are other people with powers. We call them capes, tights, and yes, superheroes. They use their powers to protect, to defend—"

The camera is still following me up. He's zoomed in, but I am a tiny figure on the screen, more of a shadow from apple-man's glowing figure.

"These heroes fight for us, they die for us, and they do it without hesitation. We don't always know who they are, but we know what they are." I can see my thrusters cut out. I shiver from the memory. I didn't really have time to think I was going to die when it happened. I was surprised when I woke up.

The sky lights up, first in brilliant white then it morphs to orange as the mushroom cloud takes shape. The camera is still tracking me. The suit is easily visible against the thermal radiation shining down. Had he detonated a few seconds sooner—

"The experts best guess based on energy signature and the size of the event, is over three million dead. This armored hero risked her life to save the city of Las Vegas." I'm still falling. My stomach goes all queasy on me. All I remember is the power going out and a few seconds later I blacked out. No kinetic shielding, no inertial protection.

"The Arizona State Militia, codename: Diamondbacks, saved the city. They fought against powerful and ruthless terrorists." A shot of Foehunter cutting down three people in a blink of an eye before slicing up Mr. Perfect.

"For Major Force. Domino, Mr. Perfect, and their newest member, Arsenal, this is what they do." There's a picture of all of us. I turn and hide my face, I can't stop myself from sweating. The photo is of me taunting Foehunter after he broke his hand on my armor.

"The city of Las Vegas hails you, the State of Nevada thanks you, and the people of the United States of America, salute you."

Kate mercifully shuts the TV off before I have to see anymore.

"You're a certified national hero! What do you think of that?" She's all smiles and shining teeth.

I grab the trash can next to the couch and I hurl my guts into it.

"You can take some time off if you want," Kate says to me. This sounds very familiar. On top of doing the PR and the marketing for the team, she also runs the schedule and the day to day operations. As far as I can tell, she runs everything but the combat operations. Luke has those because of his time in the marines. I like the guy, well, dislike him less, especially since he's been nice to me, but he isn't the most rational, clear-headed human being when the fight starts. His powers amp up with adrenaline and he becomes a fighting machine running on instinct.

"Kate, I have. I've been working in the lab nonstop since you moved me. Three weeks of R&D is enough, even for me."

Her face screws up, "You staying up until three in the morning working on your armor every night isn't time off."

I jerk my face away from the diagnostic screen I'm watching, "Are you spying on me?" Crap, I should have known...

"What? No," she starts laughing. My visage softens a little, sometimes my paranoia gets the better of me.

"I just know how you operate."

I nod. Epic signals me, he's done— the suit checks out. What I'm not telling Kate is why I'm eager to get out there. I cracked the code and now have a shiny new Zero-Point Field Module installed where my lateral power cell used to go. I've run the numbers on what it can generate, but there is a difference between what you think something will do, and what it will *actually* do. Theoretically any size field can produce unlimited energy. However, the energy has to *go* somewhere. My ZPFM is the size of a D-cell battery. More than I need to power the suit, but not too much more. If I tried to make it any bigger I would have to upgrade the suits cooling systems. They're embedded and it would require practically all new armor.

Not that I'm not already designing it. I just am not ready to go to MKII—yet. The extra power has also let me upgrade a few things on my wish list. None of which I can test unless Kate lets me back in the field.

"I appreciate your concern, honestly I do, but the best thing for me is to get back out there." I punctuate it by shaking my fist in the air.

She looks at me with her green eyes as if she's trying to read my mind. If she can she's kept it a good secret.

"She's not wrong," Luke's baritone kicks in.

"You could knock," I say sharper than I mean. He shrinks back a little. Dammit, it's not like the door wasn't open.

"Sorry," he says quietly, "But you are right. We need her out there. Since the *incident* we're getting a lot of reports of increased activity here. Central says the Riot Boys are moving this way. Pierre says his contacts are whispering about a new super-powered crew coming up from south of the border."

"We're forbidden from border security," Kate says. I didn't know that. There are a lot of rules governing how the team can be used. They—we—aren't allowed to aid the police unless specifically requested by civilian authorities. Usually we're good to go by checking with the officer in charge of a crime, but for the big ones it has to be the city or the county's top cop. We can't serve in military actions, and we can't deploy in riots or civil unrest unless it is to aid in evacuation or relief. I think the biggest deployment the Southwestern heroes usually see is in the fall during fire season.

"Why would the incident affect our powered criminal activity?" I ask.

Kate answers, "You announced yourself by saving one of the most popular cities on the planet. There is a certain kind of individual who will want to test you. See if they can break you. Some people need to know they're the most powerful kid on the block."

"So, like elementary school?"

"More like High School," Luke says.

"Fifth grade is the last one I attended," I shrug, "Well then, it's a good thing I upgraded the armor."

"Oh?" Kate asks. I smile, I will let it be a surprise. When I don't answer she smirks, "Fine then. You want back, you're on patrol in twenty, south-side route. Happy?"

I grin, "Very much so. Now, both of you out, I need some privacy to change."

Kate pushes me as she walks past, Luke just stares at me as if he wants to say something. He leaves before he musters the courage.

"Epic, seal the room."

The lights dim, reinforced shutters slide down over every window and the door magnetically locks. I'm pretty sure Luke could rip it out of the wall, but it's more for privacy than anything else.

Then I wheel myself over to the position marked on the floor. I don't know why I don't switch to a full electric chair, I imagine I could program it to do a lot of cool things. But it would be me giving up another bit of freedom. I already can't use my legs, I don't want to quit using my arms. It's enough that it wheels itself to me once I've taken the armor off.

When I'm in position the pull bar lowers down. I quickly unbutton my top and discard it. I was secretly hoping I could go out today, which is why I'm wearing my synthsuit under my clothes. My jeans are a little harder to remove and it leaves me panting from the effort. Once I'm down to just my black one piece suit I reach up and grab the bar. It slowly pulls me up until I'm extended with my feet hanging an inch from the hardwood floor.

"Initiate!"

EIGHTEEN

"You have to be kidding me? A website? About me?" I ask. It's hard to believe. Kate is talking to me over the comms, she's on monitor duty back at HQ. She's the first choice for it since she can teleport in as backup. Her powers are more interesting every day. If she's teleporting herself she can only go a few miles. If she's using her empathic abilities to lock onto someone, she can teleport across the world. To do it, she needs to have spent a good deal of time with her target. She did it for me because we seemed to have clicked. She says it is all about her emotional connection with a person.

"Seriously, I'm sending Epic the address."
Http://fullmetalsuperhero.com
"Pull it up."

The bottom corner of my HUD is replaced with the front page. Currently I'm flying a half mile above South Mountain Park, if you could call endless tracks of scrub brush and proto desert a park, trying to avoid the air traffic landing at Sky Harbor. I made the mistake of not checking in with traffic control and their shift manager ripped me a new one for a good five minutes. I get the feeling they don't like flying heroes. Especially ones who they can't see on their radar.

The web page has me on it, by me I mean Arsenal. It's a beautiful pic; I'm not sure who took it. I know exactly where it was taken. I'm crouched on the ground, one hand flat against the concrete and the other balled in a fist. It is the second before I lift off after Deadman shot me. Thinking about it makes me nauseous so I try not to. I can even see the scratch on my faceplate.

There's more than the one. Hundreds of them. Blurbs about me, testimonials from people who were in Vegas when it happened. Wow. I didn't realize how many people were at *ground zero.*

"This is pretty cool," I tell her.

"Listen, the company is sending a PR guy down here, he wants you to do some interviews, maybe pose for some detailed shots. They even want you to speak with the toy division. It could be a lot of extra money for you."

Last I looked I was worth twenty-one million dollars, money isn't a priority.

"Maybe, we'll see. Close the page Epic." The window disappears and I resume looking down at the shrub-covered hills.

My ECM master alarm flips on and I hear a tracking tone.

Infrared tracking.

"Flares!"

I see him, he's ahead of me and twenty-five hundred feet down holding a shoulder-launched surface-to-air missile. The little puff of smoke tells me it has fired and I see the exhaust as it burns toward me. Fast isn't even the right word. I throw my hands up to reverse course as Epic launches a hundred micro-flares from the sides of my legs.

I go from one-twenty to hover in three seconds. The flares keep going and the missile tracks them. The explosion peppers me with debris.

"Some idiot fired a—"

Stinger missile.

"—Stinger at me. Can I beat him up?"

"You have permission to engage, don't kill anyone. Perfect is two miles away and I'm rerouting him as backup. If you need me I can be there in a wink."

"Roger. Don't come, if they're lobbing missiles at me you won't be able to take a hit. Epic, can you see the fool?"

The little ridge the man stood on is empty. I drop down to a hundred feet and re-engage my forward thrust. At this altitude his missile won't have time to arm before it hits me.

"No time like the present to test the ZPFM. Charge IP cannons, full. Charge particle beam, full. Kinetic shields to max."

The HUD switches from the light green of patrol, to the angry red of combat. It also dims for a second as power is siphoned off to load up all my systems at the same time. I hold my breath for a heartbeat. If it's going to fail, better I know now. It doesn't. All my systems flash ready at full power. Awesome.

There's a ridge up ahead and I come around it, moving slowly. I don't want to blunder into a trap.

Of course waltzing into a trap isn't any better. There are three pick-up trucks parked with their beds facing me. Each one has what Epic identifies as a .50 caliber machine gun mounted in the back. At least thirty men are scattered around the vehicles with assault rifles. Mostly AK47's and variants, a few AR15's, and one H&K. Good for him, be individual like that.

They all open fire at once. There are so many impacts Epic is forced to stop tracking them. I cut my thrusters and land on the ground. The roar of the weapons fire is deafening, I can even hear it through my dampened helmet. I stand up and do nothing.

This is perfect. I couldn't find a better test for the ZPFM. The last time someone shot me with a fifty-cal it went right through my kinetic shielding. I watch as hundreds of rounds of ammo come to a screaming halt and fall out of the air to land harmlessly on the ground in front of me. The reading on my kinetic shield flickers between 100% and 99%.

Every round is loaded with tungsten penetrators. It is likely the fifty-cals could penetrate the thinner parts of the armor. Epic informs me.

This again. As suddenly as it started, the gunfire ends. It's followed by a clatter of magazines falling to the ground and men reloading. The fifty's are belt fed and each truck has two men in it. One is holding the breach open, the other is loading a belt.

"I don't know what I did to piss you fellas off but... would it help if I said I'm sorry?" My synthesized voice is more than loud enough to carry, but after their hailstorm of bullets I can only imagine they are all deaf.

Okay, I offered an apology. I walk forward. I could use my IP cannons but I have other shiny new things I want to—

The explosion catches me off guard and the wall of compressed air sends me flying. The shrapnel falls harmlessly to the ground, stopped by the shields. However, the concussion is transmitted through the air, my kinetic shields can't stop it. *Okay, enough of this.*

From on my butt I put my hands in front of me with my palms facing out.

"Maximum angle—fire." The Ionic Pulse cannon discharge their energy and the blue bolts fly forth striking a half dozen men. Even at wide angle they are thrown back a good ten feet to convulse on the ground.

Another grenade goes off. My kinetic field is holding at seventy percent, which is damned impressive after being hit by two grenades. It climbs toward a hundred faster than I can count.

"Epic, track and pod the grenade launcher." The *puff* of my own launcher goes off and I hear a man swear in Spanish as he lifts off the ground. He wasn't moving in any direction, the pod will take him straight up.

The fifties are done reloading as I stand back up. They roar to life along with the remaining rifles. Even under the devastating assault, my kinetic shield manages to only lose ground slowly. Maybe if they sustained it for half an hour it would quit out.

"Particle beam, safety off."

I make a fist and point my wrist at the furthest left vehicle. I have to be careful not to hit anyone. Like good little black-ops monkeys they are fairly spread out and none of them are using the trucks for cover.

I hate myself for Tucson, for having to kill anyone, but they made their choice. I'll do my best not to kill but I can't be responsible for their actions. I flex my right arm and a thick blue beam of swirling particles rips through the air, cutting the bed of the trucks at a downward angle. I move my arm to the right, dragging the blue across all three trucks. The beam shuts off and the back of the trucks slide apart where I cleanly cut them in half. The fifty cals stop firing as the barrels point down to the ground.

"Pod the guys in the trucks," I say. Epic responds with the *puff puff* of my launcher. He bags all of them in less than two seconds. It leaves me with one pod and fourteen people. My cannons are charged again. I fire, bringing it down to seven. Unlucky for them they're still firing at me. I kick in my thrusters and barrel into two, knocking them to the ground.

The remaining five, sensing it wouldn't be wise to shoot at such a close range, whip out machetes and bats and charge me. I hold my palms out and soon as they come within the cone, I fire. The sandpaper roar of my canons flattens all of them to the ground. The only thing they do is moan as their bodies spasm from the energy wrecking havoc with their nervous system.

"Domino, who do we call when a small army attacks us with military grade hardware?"

"Are you okay?" she asks.

"Yeah, I can't say the same for them. No casualties as far as I know."

"State police is en route. Are you saying there isn't anyone with powers?" she asks.

"Yep. Unless their power is stupidity, in which case I have about thirty of them."

"Epic, tell whoever it is to go away." I've been up since four am, and I'm pretty sure it's approaching ten pm. I don't know because my head is stuffed inside the chest piece of my armor. I had a stroke of brilliance this morning and I've been working on it ever since. The key is my kinetic shield and it's housed inside my chest piece. I already begged off my patrol for the day and I want to finish this.

The door chimes again.

"Fine, open," I say. I don't think anyone else in the building has voice activated controls, but it sure helps with being in a wheelchair. I hear the door slide open and large booted feet walk in.

Crud. I'm in my sweatpants and a tank top, laying on the floor with my upper body firmly ensconced in the armor.

"Amelia! Are you okay?" Luke asks as I hear him run to me. Of course he thinks I'm hurt. How could I possibly be out of my wheelchair unless I was hurt? I bite my tongue—hard—and count to five. It's difficult to say the least, when people think you are incapable of even the most mundane things.

"I'm fine, I had a really cool idea on something and I wanted to try it out."

"At eight in the morning?"

I hit my head on the upper oscillator. "What?"

"Yeah, I was coming in to go over your patrol assignment for the day and..."

I slide out from under the titanium—tungsten carbide armor. The chest piece ways about seventy-five pounds and is by far the heaviest piece.

"No kidding? Epic open the blinds." Sunshine streams in as they pull apart. I feel it now. With the fever of my work interrupted a deep weariness comes over me.

"Considering your armor is in about seven different pieces I think we can beg off the patrols until after you get some sleep."

"Actually," I say as I yawn, "what I really need is some breakfast." His eyes light up unexpectedly and for a moment I can see the man and not the marine.

"The mes—restaurant down below is five stars, would you like to go?"

My stomach growls and answers the question for me. I can't believe I spent all night installing a second kinetic shield emitter. Talk about lost in time. My wheelchair is on the other side of the room and I gesture to Luke. Without thinking he reaches down and slides his arms under me and picks me up like I'm a twig. Okay, I know I don't weigh a ton, one-fifty sopping wet, but I still open my mouth a little when his arms heave me up and it isn't even a strain for him. They're warm and comforting and I can't help but drape my own around his neck. God, he's got lines to die for. Not to mention there is something incredibly—*sexy*—about a man who can lift me so effortlessly.

We get about halfway to my chair when he's overcome with embarrassment, he goes all stiff and his face turns red. I smile. It's nice to be the one not awkward for a change.

"Sorry," he mutters as he sits me down in the chair.

"Don't be, it was unexpected but I don't mind a little assistance now and then. Give me a minute to change and we'll go." I spin around and do a wheelie down the little ramp and through the doorway to my limited living space.

I keep all my clothes in drawers low enough for me to access, everything gets folded, no hangers for me. In my old place I had plastic bins, but Kate updated everything for me. I can't say I dress quickly, but it only takes me a few minutes to switch out. I decide to leave my synthsuit here. I wouldn't put it past those dirtbags in the science division to scan it while I was out of armor. I can't imagine them trying to steal it from here, but with my alarms the remaining two members would be on them in seconds.

I roll back in and Luke is examining the suit, I would be concerned if I thought he understood any of it. He also helped save my life.

"I'm no scientist, but this," he waves his hand at the suit, "Amelia, how is this even possible?"

"Says the guy who can bench press a truck."

He shrugs. "It's a lot easier to accept super-powers. They've been around since 1903. They defy science, sure, but they have their own rules. This," he gestures at my suit, "I did some poking around on the Internet, this isn't possible."

"Not that I'm comparing myself to him, but I'm pretty sure Newton heard the same thing. Mind pushing?" He stands up and moves behind me. For such a big guy he sure has a gentle touch. We walk to the elevator in silence. It opens as soon as we get there and he pushes me inside and presses the special button.

I really hate this part. The lift shakes and I feel the energy wave pass over me. The lift suddenly runs smooth and picks up speed. I wonder, is the whole lift teleported? If so, what happens to the one back at the building. If it isn't teleported, could someone be brought in only to materialize in an empty elevator shaft and plummet to their death? Suddenly I want my armor on like crazy.

The silence drags on too long and I have to say something.

"I think every kid hopes she tests positive. I'm sure they all line up in the 9th grade and eagerly give blood to know. The truth for me is the opposite. I don't care about powers or wealth. I have—goals. I'm driven, I'm very much my father's daughter."

"If he's anything like you I would love to meet him someday."

Me and my big mouth. I can feel the tears coming and I bite my lip. The pain helps a little.

"Can we change the subject?" I don't how to ask him without sounding harsh. He stiffens beside me and nods.

"Sure. Anyway, you should know Cat-7 has requested, *repeatedly* I might add, to send a tech up to examine your armor."

I open my mouth to yell, but the expression on my face must have clued him in because he rushes to speak.

"I told them no. If you want them, you will invite them. They have no authority in our building anyways."

I try to stifle my anger, it helps he defended me.

"You should know, if anyone tries to touch the armor while I'm not in it they are going to have a very, *very* bad *last* day."

"You really don't want it out, do you?"

The door opens and the aroma of food hits me like a brick, and suddenly my mouth is watering.

"Nope, and it never will be," I look up to him, "I'm the only person in the world who knows how to make it. Once I perfected the process I memorized it, wiped all my computers, destroyed every note. Trust me, no one is ever going to figure out how I did it. Ever." I'm speaking more for Cat-7, who I know is listening, than Luke.

"Now, bacon and eggs, pronto." I jerk my head behind me so he knows to push me out. He obediently pushes me into the underground HQ. It's really quite amazing. They have enough supplies here to feed and house the fifty or so superheroes on the west coast. A map on the wall shows four such bases in the US. Portland, where we are, North Dakota, presumably in the same location as the ultramax, Miami and Washington DC.

He wheels me through to the cafe, it smells delicious. There are plenty of tables with nice linens and flowers. The ceiling is a little higher to make it feel less claustrophobic. Currently, there are a half dozen costumed heroes eating here. In groups of two and three. I don't recognize any of them, but one.

The Protector. He's probably the most well-known superhero in the world. His costume looks like he stepped out of a Greek epic, with its bronze alloy and plumed helmet. Currently he's sitting in the corner eating a stack of pancakes and reading a book. As if he can't bench press a tank.

"Luke," he waves at us as we go in. I'm not a fangirl, per se, but the Protector... I remember when he pulled a sinking cruise ship onto a beach.

"You know him?"

"Yeah, when I was on the New York team we worked together a few times. He's a nice enough guy. Kind of bookish."

He says that like it's a bad thing.

Luke parks me at a table after moving the chair and sits down across from me. The menus are pretty standard, I already know what I want, he surprises me by taking his time.

A few minutes later I'm sipping my orange juice and he's working on a cup of flavored coffee.

"Can I ask a question?"

"Sure," I say between sips.

"I mean no disrespect by this, but Amelia you literally could do and can do, anything you want. Why be a superhero?" It's good question for someone to ask. The truth is, I don't want to be a superhero. I can't tell him that, certainly not down here where our conversations are most assuredly being listened too. Our food arrives buying me a few moments. The eggs, bacon, and potatoes on my plate are cooked to perfection. Luke's stack of pancakes looks like it stepped out of a commercial.

He dives right in, slicing his fork through a pool of butter and syrup. I pick at my fluffy eggs for a moment, watching him eat. I know he works out, even though I'm pretty sure his physical strength has little to do with his muscles. How can he eat a stack of pancakes and still have a six-pack?

"I don't really see myself as a superhero I guess. I had a hard time with the codename even."

"Then why do it?"

Can I tell him the real reason? Since Las Vegas he has been kind and considerate toward me, but does that mean I can trust him? Maybe, maybe not. Certainly not here.

"I like to invent things," It isn't a lie... mostly, "I don't necessarily want to sell them. A lot of inventors in the past have made things and ran out to the world and said *look at what I made!*"

"Is there anything wrong with that?" he asks. I pop a couple of crunchy potatoes in my mouth and follow them with a sip of OJ.

"No, not inherently. Other than a lack of practical thinking."

"I don't follow?"

"Too many inventors are in such a rush to share their 'genius' with the world, they forget they live *in* the world," I say.

He still looks confused. God bless his naivete.

"Alfred Nobel felt so guilty for creating dynamite, he used his fortune to create the Nobel peace prize. He thought his creation would stop war since nobody in their right mind would actually use dynamite. Robert Oppenheimer, when he invented the nuclear bomb to end World War 2, said upon seeing it tested, 'I have become death, the destroyer of worlds'. Luke, they lived in a crazy world. Japanese super soldiers were sinking ships with laser vision, the Luftwaffe was populated by officers who could fly without planes, he had a good reason for making a weapon powerful enough that even superpowers couldn't stop it. Now, you have to ask yourself, is the world a better place for having dynamite and nukes?"

I could see him actually giving this some thought. He is full of surprises. I kick myself for just thinking of him as a 'dumb' Marine. Sure he's not me, but then again, who is?

"I would say better, ultimately."

"Possibly, we could argue that. However, I know this. If the world had access to my tech, people would die and it would be my fault. Can you imagine a tank made of my armor? Rifles firing my particle beam tech? I can. I can see it all. In the right hands maybe it can do some good. If I let it get in the wrong hands, it will most certainly do evil."

He nods and eats his food for a moment. I didn't mean for things to be intense. I get that way when I'm talking about my work. I'm glad I didn't slip up and tell him why I'm really here.

"I'm sorry about the way I treated you before," he says suddenly, "A few years ago we were in a joint action with the California team. They let anyone on their teams there. It's very...celebrity oriented."

I raise an eyebrow at that, "I thought the feds determined the regs for teams?"

He shakes his head, "Not all of them. But, yeah, a few. In Cali their team is also a reality show, I'm sure you've heard of it." Everyone has. It's the highest rated show in the country. I don't watch it, but everyone else does.

"They had this girl on their team. An archer," he says. His eyes unfocus and he gets this faraway look. I finish off the last of my breakfast and push the plate aside.

"She was a real nice girl, sweet, smart, super-talented. She had been in a couple of fantasy movies about an archer and this was the studio's way of promoting it."

Uh oh, yeah I think I remember this now.

"Anyways, we're fighting this super-powered gang. They use their powers to run drugs, sex trafficking, stuff like that. Mostly they're unregulated because they never come forward when their powers express. I was part of the team who had been asked to keep an eye on her. The fight was chaotic. Some of these guys shot energy beams from their eyes, they were serious. The fight lasted a good hour, when it was done the gang had ran. She was missing though."

I've never seen him with glassy eyes, like he was about to cry. "What happened," I whisper.

"They ended up finding her in Russia a few weeks later, after the videos came out. It was...awful. She had no way to defend herself and had no business being on a team. As far as I know she still lives in a psychiatric home. This is why I am against people without powers joining the team. It's why my first reaction to you was so negative. For that, I'm sorry."

"Oh Luke," I reach across the table and put my hand on his and squeeze. "No wonder, I would have too."

He smiles at me and we sit there. I look into his eyes and I feel a buzz in my mind, an excitement I've never really felt. With conviction I didn't know possible, I realize he feels the same way.

TWENTY

The last piece of my armor snaps into place with a click. I glance up at the status monitor, integrity checked in at one-hundred percent.

"Okay, Epic start a systems check and see if the new modifications are going to work."

"Geez, niña, you make the superhero team and you still work all the time!"

"Carlos!" I let out a squeal as I spin around. I hate when I do that, but I am excited to see him. It's been a few weeks. I roll over to him and he bends down to give me a hug.

"Is...uh, you know who, here?"

"You mean Domino?" I say casually as if I don't know why he's asking.

"Yeah, I thought I would say hi and stuff. Thank her for the keycard," he waves it in the air. It's black with the Diamondback logo on it, a triangular snake with the seal of Arizona behind it.

I smile, wheel around and roll over to the workshop, "It's pretty late, I don't think she's around. However, I could text her and have her come by..."

"Nah, it's cool. Besides, I'll be too busy kicking your butt. Where's the Xbox?"

Three hours, four cokes, and a pizza later and the problems of my life fade away. Carlos buoy's my spirits by being here. I put the controller down and stifle a yawn. Despite my usual adeptness at shooters I'm feeling my tired today.

"Okay, amigo, I'm going to let you have this one. I have to hit the sack." I wheel up the ramp. Across from my room is the bathroom, which all lay at the end of my workshop.

"You mind if I crash here? It's awful late and the buses don't run often."

"If you don't mind sleeping on the couch in the workshop," I say. I run the water for a minute and splash it onto my face. It feels good to have the cold water. I grab a rag and scrub my skin.

"Uh, Amelia..." Carlos says from the workshop. His voice sounds weird, like he's scared. I roll out of the bathroom and freeze. Vixen has her hands around Carlos neck, her claws tickling his jugular. Two men, dressed in skin-tight black suits and masks, flank her.

"A frigging cripple? You got to be kidding me," she growls. I hate that word. I may be impaired, but I am hardly crippled. I glance at my screen, usually Epic has my armor diagnostics displayed there, it is blank. Why didn't my security systems keep them out? A million questions scream through my head. I don't have time to answer any of them.

"Don't try anything stupid, girl, or I slice lover boy's throat wide open." Carlos' face is white as a sheet. I've got to do something. The two men, the suits aren't for decoration, they're some form of stealth suit or something.

"Two, get the armor," Vixen orders. As he turns I can see he's carrying a pistol that looks an awful lot like the plasma rifles. Same tech. Who are these guys?

"Listen, Vixen, let Carlos go. You can walk out of here with whatever you want. Obviously I can't stop you, and he doesn't have any powers. You don't need to threaten him."

She smiles, her canines were either elongated when she expressed or she filed them herself.

"Oh honey, I can take whatever I want, I don't need your permission. You being disabled is icing on the cake—"

The goon she called, Two, touches the control panel I keep on the side of my suit storage. Electricity snaps like a bullet and he screams as two hundred milliamps course through him into the plate on the floor. His body seizes and he collapses as the current runs its course.

"Oops," I say. I have no sympathy for murderers and thieves.

"Cute," Vixen says. She swings Carlos over to her remaining henchman and lunges at me. There's no contest, I'm in my chair, she's who she is. The wind is knocked out of me as she punches my stomach. She grabs my hair and jerks me forward, pulling me out of my wheelchair to fall on the ground.

"Leave her alone," Carlos screams.

"In case you think someone is coming, or perhaps an alarm has gone out, think again. My associate here," she points at the faceless man holding my friend, "Assures me there is a dampening field around the building. No communications, in or out." I groan, and not just from the faceplant on the floor. I was hoping Epic had gotten an alarm out. Now I know why he didn't warn me. If the rest of their tech is as good as their guns, then it is unlikely he can counter it.

"Unlock the armor and your friend can live."

I push my hands flat against the floor and look up at her. I can see in her eyes she has no intention of letting either of us live. The only question is, how smart is she? She didn't know I'm paralyzed, which means she doesn't know how I put the armor on... right?

"Go to hell," I respond. She slaps me across the face. Lines of fire burn across my cheeks where she hits. Her claws slice through my skin like ribbons. Blood seeps out of the wounds to drop on the floor. Visions of myself in the back of my parents car, helpless and alone assault me. She wraps her hand around my throat and picks me up with one hand like a vice. I cough and wheeze as I try to breathe. I beat against her forearm uselessly. My vision goes red and then black starts to creep in along the edges. I can't keep my hands up anymore.

She tosses me backward into my chair and I heave in a huge breath. My throat is raw and my limbs feel like jelly.

"If you won't do it to save you, then I will just have to slice him open, a piece at a time." Her claws whip out as she slashes Carlos across the chest. He cries out. Red blossoms on his now torn shirt.

"Okay," I cough, "Okay, I'll unlock it. Just... don't hurt him."

Carlos shakes his head, tears in his eyes, "Niña, no, she's just going to kill us anyways," he spits through clenched teeth. Good boy Carlos. Either he knows I have a plan, or he is really that brave.

As I push on my wheels for the control panel she plants a foot on my chair, "Uh-uh, no tricks. You have to be able to unlock it without being near it. I'm not letting you touch it."

I feign resignation, "Fine, there's a biometric reader on my pull bar. It's a backup."

She nods. I wheel my chair over to the bar and raise my hands. The motion sensor in the wall reads my position and automatically lowers the bar.

"Cute, the cripple likes to do pull ups. Too bad all that upper body strength is of no use to you now." I put my hands around the bar and squeeze. The pads trigger the system to rise up. When it is all the way at the top my chair rolls out of the way. I look over at Vixen, understanding dawns on her.

"Epic, initiate." They can jam wireless and they can dampen energy fields, but unless they installed sound bafflers he can still hear me. The electromagnetic field I use to keep the pieces in place, drops at the same moment my kinetic emitters fling the armor at me. In a half second I'm fully armored.

Sparks fly across the room as Vixen's claws catch me in my throat, slipping inside within the microsecond before my kinetic shields go online. My HUD flashes to life. Damn she's fast.

"Charge everything," I yell. I can't walk, I can just twist my upper body. Without my synthsuit I can't bypass the damaged nerves in my back.

She's back on me in a second, her claws out for my eyes. The kinetic shields pulse and she slams against them, all her forward momentum halted.

I throw my hand out, palm up at Carlos and his captor. Then I remember Tucson. If these are the same guys, they can somehow channel my pulse cannons to the ground. I fire a shot off at Vixen with my other hand. She dives out of the way as the blue bolt shatters my new TV and part of the wall.

With my right hand I close my fist and tilt my hand down, targeting springs to life over the man holding Carlos. I don't have time to call for his surrender. Any second they're going to threaten to kill him unless I surrender. The man reaches for his plasma pistol and I fire. The particle beam lights off, super accelerated atoms burn through the air and the man's forehead. He falls back, dragging Carlos with him.

Even if I had my synthsuit on, I'm not sure I could take Vixen. Without Epic I can't use my grenade launcher to catch her, essentially we're at a stalemate. I can't shoot her, but she can't get to me or Carlos. I can see her figuring this out a few seconds behind me. She's crouched in the corner ready to spring. Her muscles uncoil and she relaxes as she stands.

"I'm leaving," she states.

"I'm going to find you and I'm going to put you in a hole and throw away the key," I growl.

"Keep dreaming, cripple." She presses something on her wrist. Green light envelopes her and in a half second she's gone. Vanished. Teleported. Now where have I seen that tech before?

"Carlos? You okay?" No answer.

"Full sensors," I order. The rudimentary voice commands I had Epic install seem to be working, even if he can't communicate with me. They show Carlos' vitals. He's alive but unconscious.

Great. I can't walk, my face is bleeding and my best friend is out cold. It's going to be a long night.

TWENTY-ONE

I ended up having to wait all night. Whatever they used to jam the signal, it worked. I left my ECM on to see if I could get a signal out, nothing. I couldn't even sit down or I would fall over. I had to stand there, for seven hours. Thankfully the servos in my legs and hips don't move easily. I wouldn't fall over, but I wouldn't be resting.

Kate arrived first, just before seven AM. I swear, the woman complains about me being a work-a-holic, yet here she is at the crack of dawn to do PR stuff. As soon as she is within thirty feet of me I know she can feel my emotions. There's a pop and she's next to me.

"Oh my god, Amelia, are you okay?"

"It's about damn time," I reply.

Thirty minutes later I'm sitting in the first-floor conference room, still in my armor, with my back propped against the wall. I don't want out of it. Not until everyone is gone. I don't want the police arresting me and leaving my armor unguarded. All of this leaves me sitting where she left me, in the conference room with four of Phoenix's finest while they decide if it was self-defense, or if I'm a Particle Beam serial killer. They can't see my face, they don't know I'm wounded. An ambulance took Carlos out of here, they think he has a concussion, which is why he didn't wake up. He better be okay or I am going to burn Vixen to the ground.

The four uniformed officers, three men and a woman, all look between excited and nervous. I can't handle the silence anymore.

"How long have you all been on the force?" I ask not knowing what else to say. The program Epic wrote let's me speak with my normal synthesized voice.

"We're not really supposed to talk to you," the woman says, her name tag reads *Marino*.

"Really? Come on, despite what it might seem like, my suit isn't a lot of fun to be in. I haven't figured out how to put food and water in it. I'm exhausted, but sleeping is impossible inside this thing. Cut me some slack and talk to me." It's all true, no lies here. I'm exhausted, I would sleep if I could, but I can't.

"What was it like, you know, to fly up with the nuke?" One of the men asks.

"My brother is in State Police, did you really get hit by a anti-tank weapon in the mountains?" Marino asks.

"All good questions. The nuke sucked. I'm sure you all have had moments where you thought you were going to die, well it was mine. I don't know about the anti-tank weapons—they had fifty-cals loaded with armor piercing rounds, does that count?"

"Holy cow. Yeah. I was in the Army, and AP rounds on a fifty will penetrate a lot of armor, including some tanks." The one standing by the door says. He has a similar look to Luke, except smaller, more compact, and not nearly as handsome.

"Thank you officers, you can go," a man in a cheap suit walks in. He's older, maybe in his 40's, with some slight graying around his temple. From his shape he looks like he could stand to work out more. He has no trace of an accent, even though he looks Hispanic.

The officers all nod. They shuffle out of the room with a couple of smiles for me.

"Based on the weapon you described, and the telemetry from the buildings security, we're going preliminarily rule this self-defense. Now Ms...?"

"Arsenal," I say, "Ms. Arsenal if you must."

He gives me the deadpan stare. "This is a potential homicide investigation, I don't have time for your games—"

"You just said it was self-defense?" I ask. There goes my mouth again.

"The initial ruling is self-defense, but new evidence could always come to light. Now, your name?"

"Arsenal."

He's really irritated now. If he thinks I'm putting my name in the public domain, he's crazy.

"Officer...?"

"Detective," he growls.

"Detective, Arizona state law, and the US Supreme Court backs this up, my name doesn't go public as long as one named member of a team does have the information. In other words... You. Don't. Get. To. Know. Who. I. Am."

The pencil in his hand snaps and he lurches to his feet.

"This isn't over. If I find one shred of evidence you murdered these men I will have you in cuffs so fast it will make your head spin.'"

I hold out my arms. Of course I can't put the wrists anywhere near together, "By all means, slap away."

He jabs his fingers at me, "All you heroes think you're above the law. We have ways of dealing with you." He spins and storms out. I throw a mock Nazi salute in his direction, jerk.

My HUD flickers for a second as Epic connects with it.

I'm detecting severe lacerations to your face and elevated respiratory distress. Do you need ems?

"I need to get out of the armor, can you connect me to Kate?"

He doesn't respond but her voice is in my ear a half second later.

"You okay?"

"I really need to get out of this and see a doctor." A second later she pops into existence in front of me. She switched to her work clothes before the police arrived, she's wearing her form-fitting black catsuit with all her gadgets, minus the weapons, and her ID is clipped to her chest to show the police she really does work here.

"Let's get you upstairs."

Two hours later I'm sitting in the private wing of Valley Hospital. They don't know who I am, but the companies insurance covers all wounds and injuries sustained while on duty or on property. Good insurance too, I don't even need a co-pay.

The doctor is busy making *hmm* noises as he stitches up the four cuts on my face.

"It looks really painful," Kate says. She's back in her civvies.

"It isn't."

"But it—"

"The blades were razor sharp," I glance at her, "they barely even sting. I'm just glad it was my face and not my legs, that can be dangerous."

"Dangerous?" she asks.

"Yeah, I can hurt myself and not know it. Not feeling pain doesn't mean I won't get infections."

"You should be more careful Ms. Lockheart. You are correct though, the razors were extremely sharp. Any deeper and you would need surgery. As it is, if you wear the bandage the nurse will apply, keep it clean and dry, there should be minimal scarring."

"Thanks, Doc." He leaves the room. My emotional and physical strength is all but sapped. Suddenly, Kate is there engulfing me in a hug.

"I'm glad you're okay," she says.

"Me, too. Is Carlos better?"

She lets go and looks me in the eye, her hands stay on my shoulders though. Either she is using her whammy on me, or I am feeling better naturally. At this point, I don't care which.

"He's fine, full recovery and already home."

"He's going to be disappointed he didn't see you."

She shrugs.

"Sounds like he stood up bravely, I might have to drop by his house and thank him."

I laughed. If she went to visit Carlos he would about die.

TWENTY-TWO

Oh how I hate monitor duty. Until the bandage is off my face I am to avoid *excessive stress*. Which means no armor and no patrol. Which puts everyone else on patrol shifts while I sit in our command room and listen for trouble. I told Luke I could easily program an algorithm to do this and he said, "It's our duty to be there for one another."

Whatever. I could also do this from my room while I worked on my armor. He said I would be too distracted. I hate it when he's right. I get we can't trust Central, but why can't we hire someone to do this full time instead of taking a person out of the field? Granted, I would be out regardless, but in general? It doesn't make any sense. I haven't seen the budget, though. It's possible there isn't room for one. Hmm, I suppose a certain company with a planetary sounding name could donate a few full-time people. I'm sure there are plenty of qualified 9-1-1 operators who wouldn't mind a pay raise and full benefits. I make a note of that for later.

I add it to my long, long list of things which don't make sense. Like, why we haven't been assigned any new recruits from the national pool? I decided I would be a little pro-active, Luke is always complaining, though not loudly, that I don't do enough extracurricular for the team. Surely he can't complain about me checking the available heroes and maybe even sending in a request?

The problem of course, is Category-7. All the hardware is theirs. *Donated* to the teams nationwide, along with buildings, materials, etc. They're a fortune fifteen company, they have a long track record of being pro-meta, and as far as I can tell, are clean as a whistle. Other than them denying any involvement in my parents *disappearance,* they seem legit. They have tech that shouldn't exist, but they're clean.

How do I do look into them without them tracking my every move? By not using their computers. This is why I've brought my own little mainframe down with me from upstairs. It's the size of a game console, has its own built-in liquid cooling and can run circles around anything commercially available. I even built a virtual interface for it. Once I have it installed I power it on. Since I absolutely despise blinking lights, the only way to know it is on is by the slight hum. Next, I put my glasses on. They look like standard safety glasses. It was the best I could do on short notice. The world of the computers comes alive in front of me.

This is going to be good.

Now, I'm no hacker. I do have a pretty good understanding of how things work. Also, I'm plugged into a port inside the company's firewall. Technically, I'm not hacking anything.

Okay, "Epic, let's manufacture an ID. Bring up a list of their admins... Let's go with Assistant Sys Admin, Richard West, he looks like a nice fellow. Sorry Richard, but I'm sure they will figure out it wasn't you."

Epic responds in my field of vision, *Affirmative.*

It takes me all of ten minutes to crack their system and I'm in. Now to pull up the database... ah. Perfect.

Wow. There are hundreds of candidates? I quickly check the roster of the nineteen state teams. All of them are understaffed. It can't be the budget, hell they barely pay me a living wage to do this. It's no wonder everyone who can earn extra money does.

"Arsenal, are you monitoring the fire on the east side?" Luke asks in my ear.

Crap. No I'm not.

"Uh, yeah, let me give you an update."

"Epic!"

Four-Alarm fire on the 38th block of East Indian road. A propane hauler lost control and tipped over, knocking down a telephone pole. The truck exploded from the pressure build up and now the three buildings closest are on fire.

I relay it to Luke word-for-word.

"Have they asked for assistance?"

I check the log. No they haven't. I'm not sure what good Luke or Domino would be, but Mr. Perfect can do a lot with his constructs. The thought briefly enters my mind before I'm typing away, manufacturing a PFD request for Diamondback assistance, I throw Mr. Perfect's name on their specifically.

"It just came in. They're asking for any and all assistance, specifically if Mr. Perfect can come," I lie like a champ. Maybe this monitor duty thing isn't so bad.

"They asked for me by name?" Perfect interjects.

Crap, maybe they don't do that?

"Uh yeah, they say you can use your fancy magic to contain and extinguish flames," I reply.

"I never considered doing it before, but yeah, it should work. Let them know I'm on my way!"

He sounds happy. I switch freqs to PFD and open the mic, "Incident Commander 38th block, Diamondback assistance is inbound. He says he can contain any hot spots you have."

The voice which responds is gruff and hurried, "We could use all the help we can get, have him report to Chief Gomez."

I relay that little tidbit to Perfect. All in a days work for Amelia Lockheart, dispatcher.

It quiets down and I can return to my real job. If I could put my feet up on the desk I would. The Category-7 database is full of potentials, most are untrained and underpowered.

Ooh, a guy who can talk to fish, like that would ever come in handy. Here's another useless one. He can levitate. That's it. Nothing else, just levitate himself a foot off the ground. I don't know what would be worse, not having super-powers or having them and they end up being useless.

What we really need is a TK, like Harper, or a Telepath. Scratch that, no telepathy. I don't need anyone sifting through my—

Oh wow. This guy, we need him. Tony Shaw, aka Fleet. His parents immigrated here from China and he was born in Boston. Oh I'm going to love his accent! He can run at five hundred and fifty miles per hour? I do the math, at top speed he can cover eight hundred feet in one second. Wow. How is he not recruited? His other powers are all secondary to his running, he generates a frictionless field while he's moving, it extends a half inch around him. He also can turn sharp corners going as fast as three-hundred miles per hour.

He's been on the probationary waiting list for three years. He's worked as a courier in Boston, New York, and LA. Currently he's living in Minnesota. His application to the State Militia there has already been denied. Why?

Oh. I see. In field operations he consumes eighteen thousand calories a day. The average person eats a tenth of that. He has been known to consume as much as fifty. I can understand him being a problem where food isn't readily available. In a city? He's a no-brainer.

Now, how to ask for him here? I hop over to our system and pull up the interface and log in as me. Turns out, any member can request a probationary but only the team leader can sign off on full membership. Awesome. I fill out the form, request Fleet, and submit. Now, back over to my Mr. West's sysadmin login and approve the request. Done.

Now with that taken care of, I can work on the other thing. With my sysadmin access I create a little back door, a unused port and an access code for it. Next, I write a quick worm. It will siphon off information about Cat-7. A file here, a folder there, nothing they will really notice. Store it, then I can access it through the back door, download it and go over it. I can't actually have it search for anything, that would raise too many flags. I can have it scan files as they are accessed and copy them. It might take a while but eventually someone will access a file that says what happened to my parents. Especially once they know who I am.

I log out and smile. I'm one step closer to finding my parents. Also, we're terribly underhanded. A speedster will round out our powerset nicely and keep us versatile. Heck, if all he did was evacuate areas in trouble it would be worth having him.

"Arsenal?" I jump in my chair and let out a sharp scream. I throw my glasses behind my server, spin the chair around and lean over with elbow on the desk to block the speaker's view of my equipment.

"Y—yes, that's me!" I say too loud.

"I'm sorry, I didn't mean to startle you," says the man. He's in his mid-thirties, handsome if you're into movie star good looks and a gymnast build.

"I'm Sam Sykes," he holds out his hand. He's four feet away from me and I don't know what I'm supposed to do.

"Oh, sorry. That was rude of me." He walks forward and tries again. I reach up and take his hand. His shake is firm but gentle.

"I arrived via helicopter from the airport and the man in the intercom said you were on monitor duty. Is now a bad time to talk?"

I glance around at my unauthorized computer, thankful it doesn't have any lights to bring attention to it. I'm sure if the team needs me I can still respond.

"Sure," I say eagerly, "Pull up a chair."

"Thanks. This won't take but a few minutes." He grabs a chair from out in the hallway and lugs it in. While he's out I whisper to Epic, "Take over monitor duty, use your new voice."

"Affirmative," I hear in my ear. Wow, it's weird to hear him speak. I programmed him to have a masculine, gravely voice. There's this actor I love who does this mix of dark sci-fi and car racing movies and Epic sounds exactly like him. Mostly because I sampled every movie and used the audio waves to program him. Even the movie where he only says three words the whole time!

"So," I drag out the 'o', "What brings a PR minion down from on high?"

"Actually I'm the vice president in charge of PR. You don't recognize me? I'm at all the press releases and I do the TV spot. You know, *When a storm rolls into town, you need to fight fire with fire, call Category-7!*"

I nod and force a smile. "Oh yeah, sure you look taller in person."

"Thanks, I don't hear that one, usually it is the other way around!" Even with my emotional guard up he's putting me at ease. I wonder if he has powers?

"After Las Vegas you've become something of a public figure. The fact that you haven't done any interviews in or out of your armor only adds to your mystique. The only time anyone sees you is on Youtube."

Yeah I kind of like it that way. They certainly aren't getting me out of my armor and away from it for an interview.

"We would like to do a series of interviews with you, do the morning talk show circuit, maybe even a few late night shows. There's even a spot on *Studio 50,* for you. We just need to figure out the logistics."

"No," I say.

"No to *Studio 50?* It's the biggest news show in the country. More people watch that than Jeopardy!" He doesn't seem put out by my proclamation, maybe he just doesn't understand what I'm saying.

"No to the *whole* thing. I'm not giving an interview out of my armor."

He furrows his brows for a moment and takes out his phone and taps in a few quick notes.

"If it is your identity you're worried about we can disguise you. This gentlemen here," he turns the phone around it's a picture of a tall man in a mime costume.

"He's on the New York team, he can make you look like anyone else. It's the perfect disguise. Would that do?"

"Unless it's an illusion or some form of mind control, you can't hide my chair. But no, that isn't why."

He purses his lips together. "I have to say Ms. Lockheart, you're a tough one," he turns it into a smile, "but I'm sure we can come to an agreement!" He leans in a little closer. His aftershave smells amazing. I want to help him, he's so handsome and I—

Bastard. Pheromones. They couldn't physically get me so they're using sly tactics. I put my hand to my ear and fake an emergency call.

"Domino, you're in trouble? Hang on let me coordinate," I put my hand over my ear as if I'm muting the microphone in the earpiece, "We've got a passable cafeteria if you want to go *downstairs,* and we can discuss this when I'm off duty."

"I'm happy to wait here," he says with a smile. I'm sure he is. A few more minutes of his proximity in a small room and I would be putty in his hands. I nod and turn around and proceed to work on my fake call. Think! I only have maybe five more minutes. From what I understand about Kate's powers the longer you're in proximity the harder it gets to resist her.

I pull up my chat window and message Epic.

Override HVAC and turn on the heat. As hot as you can get. Open any windows you can.

Affirmative.

I feel the vibration of the furnace kick in and suddenly hot air is blowing into the room instead of cold. A dry, hot breeze rolls in from the hallway telling me Epic opened a window.

Within three minutes the only thing I can smell is the sweat in my armpits. Not to mention hot air rises. His scent is carried off to the ceiling where I hope it's harmless.

"I think there's something wrong with your HVAC," he says after a minute. I glance over my shoulder and he's taken off his jacket. Sweat stains are forming under his arms. Good, maybe if his body is too busy sweating he can't produce as much.

"Maybe you could go find maintenance for me? They're on the fourth floor. I can't leave the room." I say without looking back. I'm still typing furiously like I'm on a call and doing something urgent.

"Sure, I'll be right back."

"Can't wait!" I say with false enthusiasm. Once he's gone I fling my wheels back to the door, slam it shut and throw the lock. If I had any guilt or hesitation to go after these bastards for fear of hurting Kate or Luke, it is gone. They are going down.

"Kill the heat, Epic, before it kills me."

TWENTY-THREE

I've managed to avoid Mr. Sykes for three days now. The fourth day is the charm—for him.

"Ah, Ms. Lockheart—"

"Arsenal, if you don't mind. I'm on duty."

He grins, "Of course. Now I've spoken to your team leader and he's agreed to release you for two weeks while we do this marketing blitz."

"One second," I hold up my hand. I can't wear a re-breather around him, and I can't put on a mask, but I have a secret weapon. "Kate, can you join us in conference room three?"

She was waiting for my word and walks right in. Stunning as always she's wearing a turquoise blouse and black skirt that goes down to right above her knees. She has the right makeup on, the right jewelry, everything about her is perfect. Down to her thousand watt smile. He did say the company motto was *fight fire with fire*. Well, she's my fire.

"Mr. Sykes, it's so good to meet you, I'm Kate Petrenelli." She shakes his hand, "Wow, you've a firm grip." Did she just giggle?

"Well, uh thank you."

"I also like your taste in clothes," she takes the seat next to his and leans over to grab a glass of water. Her blouse is open enough to give him a good eyeful of her plentiful cleavage. I watch his eyes go wide and his pupils dilate. She wins. Good golly Miss Molly, I didn't know how good she is!

An hour later I've agreed to four interviews, all in armor. One in Phoenix, Austin, Las Vegas and LA. I have no real choice but to do *The Studio 50* one.

He leaves a very happy man after giving her his number and eliciting a promise from her to call. She cooed and smiled and acted all aflutter for him. She even asked his help to move a potted plant that looked far heavier than it actually was. Just so she could compliment him on his physique. In the world of emotional manipulation, Kate is Darth Vader.

"I don't understand, don't they know who you are?"

"The company? Oh yeah of course. When we sign the NDA about our base they sign the NDA about our identities. If any of our names were ever leaked or hacked, they would be out millions."

"Then why didn't he know to protect himself from you?"

"How did you protect yourself from him?" she asks.

"I went and found you. I figured you could at least keep me level headed."

She nods, "Empaths like me work on a few different levels. One, our powers literally make us good looking. I don't mean we're strong, and agile, I mean the way our body works, I could go downstairs and wolf down three bacon cheeseburgers followed a half dozen strawberry shakes and not gain a single size. I don't 'cause it's gross."

I feign disgust, "You don't like bacon cheeseburgers? I'm not sure we can be friends..."

"Cute. I do, just not more than one. Okay, so level one, looks. Level two, pheromones. We all have them, they're just stronger in an empath and we can control the ones we emit. Different scents have different effects on people. For instance, the scent I used on Mr. Sykes would, depending on the woman, have no effect, or make her irritated as hell."

I didn't feel irritated, "I guess it didn't have an effect on me then."

"I didn't think it would, unless you're into girls. I'm afraid Mr. Sykes is going to have a rather unfulfilled trip home. I've been emitting the pheromone for sex since this morning. I wanted to really amp it up and it gets stronger the longer I use it. I feel really bad for all the guys on the bus this morning, but," she shrugs.

"Okay, one and two explained, what's three?"

"Touch. My empathy is both passive and aggressive. By touching a person's bare skin I can shift their emotions toward where I want them to be. I can't outright control them. If someone is genuinely angry and furious it's unlikely I will do anything more than calm them down. But, when they're in a neutral state, I can shift it toward my liking. For him it was attraction."

"What other witchcraft do you perform?" I ask.

"Throw in basic psychology and you have a win. Men love to be complimented on their perceived strengths. He dresses nice, that one was easy, but he also works out, hence the plant. I let him do things for me because he wanted to be helpful, and I let him explain things to me because—"

"—All men love to help the ladies understand the big wide world."

"Exactly. Poor guy, he never had a chance," she says with mock sympathy.

"Which begs the question, why aren't you the head of PR for Cat-7?" I ask.

"I'm not willing to sell my abilities to improve the bottom line. On top of that, there aren't a lot of empaths. Out in the field I can do a lot of good. Behind a desk? What am I going to do, convince people to sign bad contracts? Ruin lives? No, this is where I belong." She smiles and places her hand on my leg, "I'm sorry."

"About what? You really helped me out here."

She shakes her head, "No, I'm sorry I didn't believe you. There is no reason on Earth they would send Sykes, who makes a few hundred grand in salary, here to convince you to do a few lousy interviews. None. He was here to get you away from your armor—"

"—Then they would steal it. Yeah I figured as much."

"Why on Earth would they want to kill you for it?"

"I don't know, but I'm going to figure out why, and stop them," I say with more conviction than I feel at the moment.

"You're not alone," she says. It means more to me than she could know.

TWENTY-FOUR

I'm finally back in my armor. My stitches are out and I can hardly tell I was ever cut. A week of monitor duty and I was about to go crazy. The extracurricular hacking of Category-7's computers killed a lot of the time. Now I have to wait, that's the hard part. I need to let my snooper program work.

We're all standing on the roof of our new HQ, waiting for the latest member of the team to arrive.

"I don't remember asking for this guy," Luke explains to Kate.

"He's a good candidate, Luke. Maybe there was a paperwork snafu," she replies.

"Honestly, I've been asking for new members for over a year. Ever since Stonewall left, and nothing. It's like they want us to be underpowered. Maybe they finally listened."

I try to look innocent, which is easy while I'm wearing my armor. I stifle a giggle. Maybe this is how I should do more work. I could use my own resources to hire us people to man the HQ. Right now we have the front desk man. We could use a half dozen more people, not to mention some security. How is it the teams can have access to hi-tech equipment like the hoverbikes but not other things like security?

There is an object approaching at high—

Epic doesn't get to finish. Fleet has arrived. He slides across the roof to stop in front of us, the air from his running catches up to him and blows past us like a sudden squall. Mr. Perfect puts his hands up to protect his face, Luke weathers it, and Kate simply turns her body so her hair blows behind her. I don't have to do anything.

Fleet's costume or uniform, whatever you want to call it, is awesome. His top is armless, but it isn't a tank, more like a workout shirt. It's dark blue and outlined with light blue lightning bolts that run all the way down his pants to his shoes. His outfit is skin tight, I mean *tight*. You can see every detail of his musculature. I imagine it has to be since his friction field doesn't extend much beyond him.

Kate smiles at him as the wind dies down.

"Welcome to Arizona, Mr, Shaw," she says holding out her hand. He has very Asian features, his hair is buzz cut, and the sides have little lightning bolts cut into them. He isn't much taller than me, which puts him even with the armor, and an inch shorter than Kate.

He smiles back at Kate and saunters over to shake her hand. I don't know why but I expected him to use his speed.

"It's a pleasure," his Boston accent is thick enough to notice.

He goes through the team and then he gets to me, "Wow, I saw it on the news but this is something else." I smile, even though he can't see it through my mirrored faceplate.

"Okay, you've met the team, why don't you settle in and get some rest, we'll go over the particulars tomorrow," Luke says.

Fleet shakes his head, "I don't sleep. Side effect of my powers. I'm ready to rock now. I've been waiting for this moment for three years."

Epic flashes an alert on my HUD.

There are several emergency calls at the airport. There is a man on fire attacking the planes as they take off. There may be more powered individuals but it is unclear.

"Luk—Major," I forget we're supposed to use our code names when we're in costume. Luke's costume is a very tough looking green tiger striped vest with wide shoulder straps. On the center is the Marine core logo. Under it he wears a black form-fitting long sleeve shirt. His pants are military style cargo pants with the same camo pattern as his chest piece. Boy does he love the Marines. We're certainly a drab group. Mr. Perfect more than makes up for it with his red tuxedo and black cape and top hat.

"Are you—" he's interrupted by Central giving him the same report.

"It looks like you are in for some action, Fleet. Follow my directions, don't be hasty, and remember, protecting civilians and limiting property damage is *always* the priority."

"I've had the course. Tell me what you want to do and I will play it cool," he replies. I like this guy more and more. I make a mental note to ask him what course he's talking about.

"Domino, can you port to him?" Major asks.

"We just met—so no."

"She can port to me," I tell him.

"Fleet," he continues ignoring me, "How long will it take you to get to the airport?" Major asks.

The new guy slips a GPS out of his pocket and starts to type. He's too slow for me, "Assuming three hundred is your max speed in a city, one minute thirty-one seconds. I can be there in thirty-five seconds."

Everyone on the roof turned to me. Kate's mouth hangs open and Force's jaw tightened.

"I thought your max speed was two-hundred?" Mr. Perfect asks.

"Upgrades."

Force nods, "Okay then, Fleet go and see if you can help the civilians evacuate, don't engage the hostiles." The Asian speedster nods and in a rush of wind he vanishes. I can see the dust trail heading Southeast toward the airport. Damn that's cool.

"Arsenal, go find us a place to port in, I would prefer someplace better than Las Vegas." He finishes with a grin, letting me know he's all cool.

"Everyone's a critic," I mutter. With my synthesized voice it comes off a little louder than a mutter. With my hands at my side, palms out, I engage my thrusters. The jets roar and I shoot up into the sky. In ten seconds I'm already going two-fifty. At this speed there isn't any maneuvering. Fleet would have me beat in an obstacle course. I can, however, put myself on a ballistic trajectory. I holler as I pass four hundred miles per hour. The world screams by me. Six hundred miles an hour and Epic warns me the thrusters are reaching shut down temperature.

Dammit! What did I miss? I guess no sound barrier today. I ease back the throttle and let friction and gravity slow me down to three hundred. Okay, not the thirty seconds I promised, but fifty.

I push my hands out in front of me and light off my stabilizers. My airspeed diminishes rapidly. Without my inertia field this would be a very different story. Namely, my funeral.

The airport is a mess. A jet burns at the end of the main runway, I can't tell if it ever took off or if it was sitting there. I hope there weren't any people inside. It's an inferno. Several fire trucks have been knocked over, along with come baggage carts.

I land on the roof of the tower and scan the field. Epic flashes Fleet's location at me. He can do better than three hundred. Must be because there is a lot of open ground in Phoenix. He's twenty seconds out.

"I'm here," I say over the radio. "Bring up all our active sensors and let's see if we can pinpoint these yahoo's." Epic complies and a stream of sensor data pours onto my HUD. "Epic, we need cameras too, this is too big a deal to not put all our cards on the table."

All it would take would be for these guys to bring down one loaded jumbo jet and it would be a disaster. I hear two rapid fire pops and Force is next to me. He has his binoculars out, scanning. We're on the team only, encrypted channel, which means I can speak freely.

"Epic will have us cameras in a second," I tell him.

"Who's Epic?" Fleet asks as he runs through the tarmac and up the side of the tower to stop next to us.

"A hacker we use on the side," I lie.

"Cool," he says out loud. Another pop and Domino and Mr. Perfect arrive.

The systems are encrypted by a Federal firewall. I can break them but I will be detected.

"Epic's having trouble, we're going to have to find another way," I tell them.

Fleet, search the place, but don't engage," Force tells him.

He grins and vanishes with a puff of air.

"Who do we know who can control fire enough to burn?" asks Domino.

"Any ideas, Arsenal?" Force asks me.

"I found them," Fleet says, "and I mean *them*. Six powers, fire guy, a big dude who looks like he jacked too many steroids, some cowboy, a hot chick with an energy sword, a guy who looks like a mummy, and a guy on a flying carpet."

"Fleet, return to me—"

A blast of wind hits us and Fleet is here.

"They look dangerous," he says as he peels open an energy bar and starts eating.

"Epic?" From the looks Domino and Force are giving each other I'm not sure I'm going to like the answer.

The Psychotic Six. They're listed as being in the North Dakota UltraMax. No news reports of them escaping have been filed. They are extremely dangerous. Lethal force would not be inappropriate.

"It's the Psychotic Six," I inform them.

"Force—" Domino says.

"—I know. We're outgunned here. Central," he puts his hand to his ear. "Central?"

"Epic are we being jammed?" I ask.

No. The comm channel is open, no one is responding.

"I'm getting a bad feeling of deja vu." It's like Las Vegas all over again. Who wants us to fail? And why? We should never have been sent to Las Vegas, and now the *single* most dangerous group of psychos to ever have powers just happens to show up in Phoenix? I can't even do math that crazy.

"We're on our own... again," Force says, "We can't let them run free, they're murdering psychopaths. If New York had the death penalty they wouldn't even be alive after what they did."

"I'm more concerned about the here and now," Domino adds, "One or two of them we could handle. But all six?"

Force glances down at is feet, I can tell he's at a loss for words. He's great in a fight, something he can wrap his hands around, but problem solving and tactics aren't his thing.

"Epic, show me the opposition and go on comms."

His voice comes over our earpieces and it sounds awesome, I know the situation sucks but if Central is offline we need something to help us.

"Bandit has a power set similar to Deadman, extremely high visual acuity. He is also inversely invulnerable to the force applied to him," Epic says in his cool new voice.

"Which means the harder you hit him, the less it hurts him, great," Domino mutters.

"Blade," Epic continues, "wields a sword made of plasma energy. It defies science and can cut through anything. Including you, Arsenal. Sandman is a sand elemental, a living sandstorm. Jadoo, is similar in power to Mr. Perfect, he is a mage and can control matter."

"He's nothing like me. My power comes through study and practice, he's a fraud who sacrifices life to power his black magic."

I've never actually seen Perfect mad before. If the situation weren't horrific I would smile.

"Tire-Iron is invulnerable and a F5 strongman. Finally there is Nova. He's an F4 fire generator. His flames can melt most steel and reach as high as two-thousand degrees—"

"—Thank god for small favors," I say.

"—He can also fly and project it like an explosion."

I don't think any of us have anything witty to say after Epic's rundown. Several F5's, killers and psychopaths.

"Okay, we go in hard and fast, hit them before they even know we're there," Force says slapping his hands together. I glance at Domino and her expression mirrors my own. It would be suicide to hit them head on.

"Force," I say with my synthesized voice, "Head-on may not be the way to go here. We haven't exactly had time to work as a team. When we fight we all tend to pair off and fight people one-on-one."

I can see his hackles are up. The man is ruggedly handsome, but when his powers kick in he's brutish. Not his fault, I know, but it is weird to see the guy who's sweet and nice to me sometimes, become a rage monster.

I hold my hand up to forestall his complaints, "Listen, focus for a second. There are five of us and six of them. I can't fight Blade and you can't take Tire-Iron. Unless you can get angry enough to go F5?"

He shakes his head, his lips are pursed hard together. I notice Domino has her hand on his arm, good girl.

"Okay then, I think I have a plan, but you all are going to have to trust each other, and when Epic tells you to do something, do it without hesitation? Are we clear?" I can't believe I'm speaking to these people who have all been doing this a lot longer than me as if I know what I'm talking about.

Domino takes her hand off Force's arm and puts it out palm down. It seems a little hokey, but I'm in. I follow her lead. The rest follow me.

"There are people down there who need our help. We save them, stop the bad guys, go home alive," Domino says, "Now let's kick their ass."

TWENTY-FIVE

The Psychotic six have rounded up a hundred or so people and are holding them hostage in the baggage claim of Terminal six. Anyone of them could kill ten or fifteen hostages before we could stop them. The trick is to remove the hostages from the equation. The bad thing about baggage claim is the walls are almost all glass, with three sets of doors on either side leading to underground parking. There isn't any way for us to approach without being spotted. The good thing about baggage claim is there are seven entrances they didn't think to cover.

Carousal seven is on the far northwest corner and offers me an almost perfect view of the whole room. I'm using a detachable wi-fi cam I borrowed from one of the pieces of luggage and I put it right outside the rubber shields. I can see four of the psychos, the only ones I can't see are Tire-Iron and Nova, and I'm pretty sure they aren't sneaking up on me.

One hundred and three hostages, twenty-six of which are under the age of eighteen.

"Awesome," I whisper in my helmet. I have no need to whisper, Epic is fantastic at knowing when I'm talking to him or people outside, but it feels like I should.

"Force, twenty-six kids, they're the priority."

"Why is it always save the kids, as if adults have nothing to live for," Fleet breaks in. "Because," I try to remember he's the new guy and not sound angry with him, "Any parent would want you to save their kid before you saved them."

"Oh, yeah I guess that makes sense."

"Kids first, Fleet. When you grab someone, does your inertia field immediately engulf them or do you have to stop for a minute?"

"I've got to stop for a second. All I need to do is hold them *before* I start running and the field protects them." I do some math, he can literally traverse the terminal six times in one second. The trick is, he has to stop to pick people up. For a brief moment it makes him vulnerable. Well, it's this or go home.

"Cops and Feds are here," Domino breaks in. She and Force are topside to greet them. If I give the go code she'll port him to me then follow with Perfect. Fleet's only job is to rescue civilians, a perfect use of his powers.

"Epic, turn on the AC." Now that we're inside the building we have a little more control, still can't tap the cameras, unfortunately. Who knew the airport would have tighter security than a multinational Fortune fifteen company?

I hear the distant hum of machinery as the HVAC kicks in. Cold air blows into the baggage area. Hopefully it's enough to mask Fleet's speed gusts.

"Arsenal, there's a Fed here who wants to know what they're doing?" Force asks.

"Nothing, each of them are standing around like they haven't a care in the world. The only person who looks antsy is Blade, she's marching back and forth snapping her sword on and off. Force, do we go? If they decide to start killing people..." I don't even want to think how many will die.

Long seconds stretch by. Visions of Blade lopping off people's limbs run rampant in my mind. I can't fathom why we wouldn't go, but if the Feds are here maybe they want to negotiate. If they do, it could cost us the element of surprise. Nothing in any of their records suggest a probability of a successful negotiation. This isn't some desperate loner who was caught robbing a bank and wants a way out. These six people are hardened criminals and mercenaries. They murder, maim, and kill, all before breakfast.

"The AIC wants to try talking first," Force growls.

"Epic, distortion mode." I wait a second for him to kick it in. "What did you say? Do we go?" To Force it will sound as if there is interference. I can always say the HVAC system jammed me up. I don't care what the Feds want to do. This isn't what it seems. It smells like a setup, again. Like Las Vegas there is a potential for a whole lot of innocent deaths. We're heroes, we can't let it go down like that.

"I said don't go," Force growls.

I pretend like I don't hear every word, "Go? Roger that. Fleet, we have a go," I say to him, then to Epic, "Cut off Force's comms for a moment."

Affirmative.

"No I said—" and the line goes dead.

"Arsenal, do I go or stay?" Fleet asks.

"Last word I heard was go."

He knows the deal and so will everyone else. This gives Force plausible deniability, but everyone else on the comms heard. Lucky for me it's encrypted *by* me.

"Okay, say when."

I turn it over to Epic, he's the one who can do the math far quicker than I. He tells Fleet exactly which person to grab before he starts. To keep things precise he switches to a sharp half-second tone to tell Fleet when to go.

The first one goes off. Fleet appears in front of a woman, grabs her and the baby she's holding and disappears in a blur of speed.

"Turn Force's comm back on," I tell Epic.

"Don't go, dammit! Arsenal, respond!"

"Oh, I heard go, we've already got one." I hear a commotion over the comms, it sounds like a crying baby.

"Fleet dropped her off," Domino breaks in.

"It will work, boss," Fleet says, "I can do this."

"Luke, if we want to play it by the book, you can declare this a state emergency by the Militia Act. If the FBI wants to wrest jurisdiction from us they'll need to get a warrant."

Another tone goes off. Fleet blurs into existence in front of a little girl and her younger brother. He heaves them both into his arms and vanishes. He took too long, but it doesn't look like anyone noticed. I make sure to capture the stream of tears on the dads' face. I'll show Fleet later and then he'll get it.

"Arsenal, are you sure? We could go to jail," Domino says, "I've never heard of this law."

I chuckle, "Article twenty-six, title five-oh-seven. Tell him to read a book."

Another tone. Fleet's in and out with another kid. This could work. There's one, tiny flaw in our plan. Eventually they're going to notice they don't have as many hostages as before. They may not all be sharp, but they're not stupid either. I check the power levels. Everything is charged, and my secondary kinetic emitter is at full power for my new surprise. If I have to alpha strike them I'm pretty sure I can hurt them.

Another tone. Fleet appears in front of a young man. Oh god, no. The boy's autistic and starts screaming when Fleet grabs him. He disappears in a blur but the damage is done.

"Supers," the Cowboy yells.

"Kill all of them," Blade yells as her sword snaps into existence. I don't know if they mean us, or the hostages, but I'm not going to find out.

"Full power thrusters," the jets kick in and I burst through the carousel, "Backup now!" I scream into the radio. Fleet is a godsend. I see him blur in and take another hostage. I raise my arms to Blade and fire a full power cannon charge at her. She raises her sword and the blast wave deflects around her. I did not know she could do that!

Force is there roaring suddenly, he's much bigger as he charges Cowboy. The man in a ten-gallon hat quick draws two five hundred magnum revolvers and blasts away at the ex-Marine. The bullets hit with enough power to penetrate a car block. Unbelievably, Luke spins sideways to avoid the first two. I don't know how he knew Cowboy was going to fire, but he did.

I land between the largest group of hostages and the killers in the room. My arms are out wide as I try to cover everyone as Fleet whips in behind me and rescues a hostage every three seconds.

Jadoo and Blade rush me. He's waving his hands and chanting and I can see the power rolling off of him, but Epic has nothing on our sensor suite.

"Kinetic Lance, fire!" With the ZPFM installed I can keep all my weapon systems charged. The beam of pure kinetic energy smashes against an invisible barrier I didn't know the mystic had. I jump left as Blade's sword cuts through the space I occupied a moment before. I hear a pop and more chanting. I can't take my eyes off Blade to see what is happening.

"You come here to your death, stupid girl," she says as she charges me. Yeah, I'm not playing this game. "Thrusters." I lift off and go up fifteen feet, I'm glad they have high ceilings. I take three seconds to spin completely for Epic to know what's going on. Mr. Perfect and Jadoo are locked in a blaze of psychedelic energy as they both try to annihilate the other.

Force is punching Cowboy hard enough to push the man through the concrete pillar he was standing in front of. The important point is his guns are on the ground. Domino is teleporting in rapid succession around Sandman slashing away at his wrappings with a blade I didn't know she had. He's shooting blasts of sand at her but she's not there to receive them.

Epic puts the number of hostages remaining on my screen, *87.*

I lay eyes on Tire-Iron and Nova, they're at the far end, away from hostages where the police would have come in. I'm out of time to look around because I hear Blade behind me. I jet forward clumsily and spin around, she leaps up and slashes at me with her sword. The plasma blade sparks as it cuts a two-centimeter gash through my chest piece. Luckily it's the thickest part of the armor - I can take it.

"Epic, I really need to not be fighting her."

Thirty-five degrees to your left, full power thrust.

I do it. I blast away from her just as Force charges past me. It's insane how agile he is when he's big and strong. It's like he knows when to dodge without even seeing the blow. I hope he fares better against her than I did.

I slam into Cowboy at seventy miles an hour and crash him into the concrete wall behind him. It spiderwebs and mortar and dust fall on us. I'm pretty sure he's okay, since he can theoretically be invulnerable to anything.

I push off and level my cannons, they're reading one-hundred percent, and fire. The blast of Ion energy rips through him and slams him back down to the ground from where he was almost up. He may be invulnerable to physical attacks, but he still has a nervous system.

"Pod him," I hear the *puff* of my grenade launcher and he floats unconscious up to the ceiling.

"One down."

The number on my screen changes to *76*. I guess without him having to wait to go he can move a little faster than one every three seconds. At least all the kids are out. I don't know how to deal with Sandman, and Mr. Perfect and Jadoo are surrounded by bizarre energy which could disrupt my armor, I can't risk it.

"Major Force, Domino, trade," Epic says over the comms. Domino, like a champ, teleports to Force, slaps her arms around him and appears next to Sandman with him. Then she's back to Blade.

Engage Nova and Tire-Iron before they have a chance to return to the hostages.

Two on one and they're both deadly.

Awesome.

The thing about superpowers, is they seem amazing until you fight someone your powers have no effect on. I blast down the baggage claim to the east end where the two most powerful members of the Six were waiting to ambush any police who came in. I land fifteen feet from them with my arms up to fire my cannons. I suspect it won't have an effect on Tire-Iron. The big lug steps in front of Nova and the energy wave dissipates off of him.

"Tire-Iron, Blade failed, do you think you can take her?" he asks in his creepy crackling voice. I'm not sure if he's surrounded by fire, or is living flame. It's hard to tell. The floor under him is black but not burning. My sensors register him at three hundred degrees.

Tire-Iron leers at me, "I'm gonna rip you out of that armor and break you in half." I fire my cannons again. Okay, he should not be fast and strong. I hear glass shatter and then a roar like a campfire and Nova is gone.

Running? It doesn't seem like the thing to do.

"Epic, all power auxiliary kinetic fields."

This isn't exactly the test I was hoping for. Tire-Iron lumbers toward me and I stand my ground. Five-eight in the armor and he has to be six-six. He towers over me.

"And they said you were smart," he rears back his arm. Did he just imply he was warned about me? I don't have time to guess. His fist is nearly the size of my head. He lets fly, I reach up with my left hand—and catch his fist. A thunderclap blows through the room shattering windows and sending debris flying. My design worked, I'm holding his fist.

I'm glad I'm recording the look on his face.

"What?" he asks.

"Yeah, it's like that," I put my right hand against his knee and bend my wrist down while flexing. Time to see how 'invulnerable' he really is. Sub-atomic particles charged with positive energy and accelerated to near light speed fire out of my wrist emitter in a howl of fury and fire. The beam splashes against his knee and for a brief moment I think it isn't going to work.

Then it cuts through and blasts out the other side.

His mouth opens and his eyes fill with tears. The man mountain who's committed countless crimes, falls down grasping his knee and keening like a little baby as tears and snot roll down his face. There are days I love my job.

"Pod him." *Puff* and he's floating up. I imagine he could do some damage to the ceiling, even get through the roof, but all he would do is float away.

Domino has Blade in a choke hold and is riding her down like a calf. I can't hear what she's saying but whatever it is, the swordswoman is slowly relaxing. The plasma sword vanishes and she drops to the ground unconscious.

Perfect and Jadoo are still locked in their battle and I take an educated guess. "Fire kinetic lance," the force beam smashes into the man on the carpet and crumples him like a rag doll. With his concentration broken, his energy constructs vanish and Mr. Perfect's power crashes into him. A smoking husk of burning flesh and scorched hair falls to the ground.

"I don't know how to fight this thing," Force screams. Sandman is the only one left besides, Nova. I step forward to help when Epic flashes a warning on my screen.

Temperature outside is spiking. There are tens of thousands of gallons of jet fuel in and around this airport. Nova could detonate it and cause a catastrophe.

Done, I turn my back on my team, hopefully they can finish this and I kick in the jets. My armor blasts through the nearest window and I'm up in the air at a hundred miles an hour, banking to the West scanning for Nova.

"Epic, these guys acted like they were ready for me. Come to think of it, Blade seemed pretty fixated on me. Who could sneak these monsters out of prison and move them to Phoenix without anyone noticing?"

It would require contacts inside the North Dakota UltraMax. As well as some form of technology or power to move people undetectable across the breadth of the nation.

"In other words—"

Teleportation.

"Yeah. Why am I not surprised. Same with Vixen and this supposed *cabal*. I've had enough of this crap – when this is done we're going after the source."

Epic locks onto Nova's position. He's floating a hundred feet above the fuel storage. Jet fuel burns at fifteen hundred degrees. The HUD says eleven-hundred and I'm five hundred feet away.

"Will the cannons work on him?"

Unknown. Heat can disrupt ion-particles. "This really is Las Vegas again. At least he can't melt the suit."

I aim for the center of the fireball and I dive in. My faceplate immediately goes dark to protect my vision. I slam into something. He screams and I wrap my arms around him.

"I will burn you to a cinder!"

"Bring it, but I hope you brought your own oxygen supply."

"What?"

"Epic, full power, ballistic trajectory straight up."

The thrusters will overheat.

"He doesn't know that." The jets on my back, the sides of my boots and the one on the hand that isn't wrapped around him, all light off with intense force. I hear the sound of a rocket blasting through the sky and I realize it's me. He screams and the temp on the HUD flares to thirteen hundred. We hit four-hundred miles per hour and the overheating alarm starts blaring.

"Punch it!"

The afterburners kick in and we rocket past six-hundred miles per hour. He stops screaming. Warning lights are flashing all over my HUD.

"Cut power, let's fall." The thrusters shut off and wind down and I'm falling. My faceplate clears and I can see again. Nova is unconscious, frost covers his skin and I think I might have broken all his ribs. Whatever, he made his bed. The HUD says we're at seventeen thousand feet. "Hot damn, Epic. I need to work on the overheating issue. I want us in space. Wouldn't that be—"

Awesome?

"You read my mind."

TWENTY-SIX

It's weird being on a stage while thousands of people cheer at you. Plain weird. The crowd is huge, I only know exactly how many people are attending the celebration because of Epic. He kindly lets me know. I'm not sure if this is his idea of a joke or not. I hate crowds and if I wasn't in my armor I would be rolling for the hills. Regardless, I have a running ballistic course set in for the HQ.

We're all here. It wasn't a request. The mayor of Phoenix called Luke personally and asked for us. I think they like the fact that we stopped the Psychotic Six with no civilian or police casualties. Nova succumbed to his injuries and I'm trying real hard not to feel bad about it.

I've prepared for this my whole life. Mentally, at least. Physically... I've watched a lot of movies and read books on tactics and fighting. Until three months ago I had never so much as had an argument with someone. Not in real life anyway. I argued plenty with a so-called 'scientist' at Harvard and MIT, over the Internet anyway.

Now I've killed people and severely crippled many, many more. Is it irony? A crippled person crippling other people? I shouldn't feel bad for Tire-Iron, he had it coming and if he can never walk again, well then maybe he'll never kill again. I shake my head, no, I did right. *Then why do I feel guilty about it all?*

Kate puts her hand on my shoulder, she must be feeling some backlash from my inner turmoil. They caught me by surprise when they showed up today in different uniforms. Had I known we put on colorful, flashy outfits for public appearances I would have added some flashing lights or something.

Kate's wearing a dark blue semi-rigid top. It looks like body armor. Under it she has on a form fitting long sleeve shirt and below it a skirt. I couldn't believe it. She's wearing a skirt. Her boots come up to her calves and she has stockings on for the rest but...

Luke's wearing something I could best describe as a Marine dress uniform without any medals or insignia. Fleet's never had to make a public appearance before. He didn't have time for an alternate costume. Kate set him up with a very nice metallic blue suit. He wore his usual domino mask as did Kate. Luke had his half-mask on and Mr. Perfect... he wore a tux. Which is totally normal for him. Along with his Phantom of the Opera mask. He twirled his little cane and smiled and all the ladies swooned. What is it with him?

The stage is large enough we can all stand shoulder to shoulder with plenty of room. Right now the Chief of Police is recounting his experience of how Fleet saved child after child and even brought a mother with her baby.

He's last in line on my right, we're formed up in order of seniority, and I nudge him.

"See," I whisper.

"Yeah, yeah, I get it, women and children first."

The ceremony goes on for a while, finally culminating in the Mayor giving Luke an award for the whole team. The crowd cheers and we all take a bow. I almost missed my cue. Halfway through I started falling asleep. I put Star Trek on my heads-up display to help keep me up. I think Kate noticed my mood change because she gave me some funny looks.

I can't help it, I love me some Captain Kirk.

The cheering goes on and on. I wave a few times and then it is over. Kate guides us down the stage to the waiting crowd for autographs and pictures.

"I'm sorry, I can't really hold a pen." I'm going to hell for all the lies I tell. "I'm happy to take a picture with you." I tell one young lady. She poses as her parents snap a pick.

Kate nods at me, or past me, and I turn and look. My heart stops. There's a little girl in a wheelchair. She can't be more than eight or nine. She's hanging back from the crowd. It's rough in the chair. Crowds are an opportunity to be accidentally knocked over, or pushed in a bad direction. I had to weigh every crowd, every line, and decide was whatever I was doing worth the risk?

I could see her doing the same math and deciding against it. I couldn't take it.

"Excuse me," I begged off another photo op and walked toward her. I'm not tall, not even in the armor, but I am bulky. I don't think anyone would miss me in a crowd.

Her face lights up as I walk to her. I don't see her parents, but I can't imagine they aren't nearby. I kneel down in front of her to look her in the eye while we speak.

"Hi, I'm Arsenal." I don't think I've ever wanted to open my faceplate more than right this second. Stupid secret identity.

"I'm Wendy, I can't believe you came over here. You're my favorite!"

I smile inside my helmet. I have a fan.

"Wendy, can I tell you a secret?" I lean in as I speak. Her face lights up and she leans closer.

"I'm in a wheelchair too," I whisper. I don't think her eyes could get any bigger without falling out.

"Really?"

"Honest Abe." I say holding up my hand, "I invented my armor to help me walk. Only when I'm in my armor, the rest of the time I wheel around just like you. "

She reaches out and touches my arm, "If I had this I would never leave. I miss running something awful." I'm desperately trying not to cry.

"I do too. I can't stay in here all the time—it smells if I'm in here too long."

She laughs. I reach over and hug her as best I can and she hugs me back.

"You're my best friend," she whispers in my ear.

"Our secret, okay?" She nods. Her mom picks that moment to walk up on us. I watch as she wheels Wendy away. The little girl glances back every few seconds and waves. I wave back every time.

I don't know how long I'm standing there watching her go. If I do nothing else in life, this moment will have made it all worthwhile. I didn't have anyone to look up to as a kid, I just wanted my family back. Maybe there's more to this business than flying around stomping bad guys. I never had a ton of respect for them before, but maybe I was wrong?

"Arsenal?"

I turn around and come face to chin with Luke. He's smiling. The skin around his eyes crinkles just a little bit from his squinting. It's Arizona after all, and their costumes aren't equipped with self-polarizing lenses. Which gives me an idea.

"Epic, make a note, let's look at re-vamping their costumes."

Note made.

"Neat, huh, when you can inspire people?"

I forget he can't see me smile. "I didn't know about this part, you know? Saving lives, sure, but inspiring people?"

"Most of us are forced into this. Our powers express and we're too young to know what to do or too scared."

"Which were you?" I ask.

He looks far away, not to the distance, but in the past.

"A little column A, a little column B, I suppose. The way my powers work, well, when I was a teenager you can imagine the problems I caused. Joining the Marines helped, but not as much as I would have liked."

His sudden open nature catches me off guard. I wish I wasn't in my armor. I want to touch him.

"I guess what I'm trying to say is, being a leader is terrifying. I'm constantly afraid of making the wrong decision, of causing someone's death. All that. Here you come along and you always know the right thing, you always have your head on you. There are days I don't even know why the Arizona AG put me in charge."

He pauses for a moment, looking down at his feet. He doesn't like being in charge, that much is obvious. Being terrified of it was less so.

"When we're in the field, like we were against the six, and I... don't know what to do. I want you to take over. I may not be a good leader, but I'm good enough to let others help. Okay?"

"You got it... boss man."

He cringes, but he does smile.

TWENTY-SEVEN

"Can I come in?" asks Luke. My workshop is a *mess*. I have parts strewn everywhere and my new project is in a four-foot long metal box rigged with a kinetic field generator. I would have gone back to Detroit where I made the suit in the first place to do this, but I don't have the time, and I don't want those bastards at Cat-7 to know anything about how I built the suit.

I'm dressed in shorts, a tank top and my welding gloves as I solder a connection together under a microscope. My black hair is pulled back with a rubber band and I have these enormous goggles on. I'm the picture of beauty.

His unexpected emotional outburst, in a good way, has me reeling with chills every time I think of him. The way he opened up to me was wholly out of character for him or at least the character I had come to expect from him.

I wouldn't care as much if it weren't for the fact that he is *exactly* my type. Tall, smooth skin, and a smile to die for. And his eyes... I could lose myself in his blue eyes.

"You there, Amelia?"

"Oh, yeah, uh, yeah." I say smoothly. I was staring, great. I pull off the goggles and free my hair from the rubber band. A quick dash of my hands through my hair and I look marginally better.

"What can I do for you, boss man?" He smiles at my cheeky remark. I know he doesn't like it, but maybe he's come to tolerate it from me. Since the other day I've felt a tad bit awkward around him. Kate assures me it's perfectly normal to be awkward around a person you like, especially if they like you back. I told her she's out of her mind.

"What are you working on?" he asks, deftly avoiding my question. Of course he knows I can't resist talking about my projects. I give him my best wry grin.

"You certainly know how to play me. I can't resist, though!" I rub my hands together with glee. It's good timing on his part because it's about done.

"I didn't make the armor in my backyard, I had to go somewhere specialized to do it."

"Where?"

"It's not important. What is, is that I can't go back, not with Cat-7 watching me. Even though the armor is theoretically indestructible it is entirely possible I might have to fabricate a new part. When I first purchased the raw materials—"

"Wait, you bought titanium?"

"Military grade titanium, it ain't cheap. Same thing with the tungsten carbide, and I needed a lot too. It's not like the suit is a single piece of—why are you looking at me like that?" His mouth was open and his eyes were wide. He shook his head for a second and ran his hands through his buzz cut. He always did that when he was thinking.

"Would you mind if I came in and sat down?"

"Be my guest." He closed the door behind him and to my surprise, sat on the floor in front of me. Luke is tall enough even when he's sitting. It's an odd experience for me. He's 6'4" when we're not fighting and with him sitting cross-legged on the floor in front of me he has to look *up* at me while I'm in my chair. I don't think he could have done something more respectful and nice, if he had tried.

"Thanks, now, go on?"

"Where was I?" Damn I lost my train of thought. I seriously need to stop staring at his eyes—

"You were talking about buying military grade alloys."

"Right, I needed a lot. My calculations were perfect, but the actual practical application of the process could need refinement. In other words, I had to try a few times to get it right. Also, I couldn't be sure of the availability of it in the future. I bought— enough. Thankfully, I haven't needed to make any new parts. After our fight with the Psychotic Six I started thinking maybe I didn't have all my bases covered when it came to weapons." I'd also needed a tiny amount to reinforce my chest piece after Blade nearly penetrated it.

He chuckled, "Your name is, Arsenal. Making new weapons seems like the thing you would do."

I can barely keep myself contained as I spin the chair around to look at the readouts. I only need a few more minutes.

"Yeah, but I want to show you, not tell you."

"Fair enough. Mind if I ask a question?"

"Shoot." I'm fiddling with a dial when he asks. I know the pressure is right, but it helps my nerves to double check.

"How much are you worth?" he asks. I freeze, I really should learn to keep my big mouth shut. It isn't like it needs to be a secret, but the more people know about me, the more I know about them, and then what if they're somehow involved?

"Would you let it go if I said, a lot?" I hunch my shoulders hoping he can read my body language.

"Of course. I was just curious because you've never requested any parts or equipment with your per diem. Kate paid for all of the computers in here with our discretionary fund. Except, for Epic of course."

I roll back over to him, a little closer than is strictly necessary. His eyes light up as I lean in, "I invented a little device which will help jets become much sturdier during high-g turns. Lockheed bought it from me for a tidy sum and Epic has been playing the stock market with what was left after I bought everything I needed, ever since."

"So," he says with a smile, "you're a genius, you're rich, and you're beautiful? How are you not married?"

I laugh, of course he's joking. What guy in their right mind would want a small-chested paralyzed girl who may not even be able to have children? No one, that's who—he's not joking. I'm laughing and he's not. He's serious. Suddenly the temperature in the room is far too much for me. My stomach clenches and my mouth has turned into the Sahara.

"Well, uh, that is—um." Super genius with science, super idiot with words. We're still close together and he leans forward. His head tilts to the side and—oh god he's trying to kiss me. I don't know what to do.

"This is the part where you lean forward, or slap me in the face. It could go either way," he says with his sly grin.

I laugh nervously and decide to lean forward. Our lips meet and electricity leaps between us. An emotional wall I've been holding back my whole life, cracks. I put my hand on the back of his neck and I push hard against him. Our mouths open and for the first time in my adult life, a man is kissing me.

It's incredible. My heart is beating so fast it feels like a rabbit is kicking me from the inside. I'm warm and cold at the same time. Things stir below my stomach I never expected to feel. Things I didn't *know* I could feel.

Distantly, I'm aware of an alarm clock going off. Why would I set an alarm—oh, it's ready. Reluctantly, I break the kiss in a way that isn't sudden or off-putting. I lean my forehead against his and our eyes are mere centimeters apart.

"Wow," he says, "I was worried you were going to go with the slap."

I try to play coy but it comes out as sarcasm, "I still might." Thankfully, he laughs. I want to kiss him again, in fact, I think I want to do more than kiss him. Oh, my alarm, right.

"Okay," I push myself away and wheel over to the computer. My ears are warm and my stomach won't stop moving around. It was just a kiss... what a kiss!

"Are you ready?"

He nods. I hit the button lowering the kinetic field within the grey-silver box. It's made out of a grade of titanium that is *extremely* pressure-resistant. Not the same stuff I use on my armor, but close. The box opens down the top and folds to reveal my brand new, four-foot long sword. The blade is black with the gray of the carbide on it. The cutting edge sparkles from the crushed diamond coating.

"Holy crap, that is the prettiest thing I've ever seen!" Oh good, he likes it. I haven't fastened on the hilt yet, the blade just ends in the tang.

"The core of the blade is titanium, of course, which I've bonded tungsten carbide too. It's as strong and as hard as my suit. The blade..." he reaches out to touch it and I lurch forward, "Don't!" He freezes.

"Uhm, the blade is coated with diamond powder which has been compacted to a monocrystalline form." I explain hurriedly.

"Uh, Amelia, I don't know what any of that means."

"The edge is one molecule of diamond crystalline thick. It literally can cut through anything, except itself."

His jaw drops and he looks at me. The admiration I see in his eyes makes all of this worth it.

"I think this deserves another kiss," he says. I can't say I disagree with him.

TWENTY - EIGHT

The hilt of the sword had been a little trickier than I originally thought it would be. I didn't account for the amount of force I would be swinging it with. On my first practice it shattered. Which is bad considering what's in it. It got me thinking, which is why I'm up at seven in the morning with my magic box.

The kinetic field emitters inside the apparatus are busy compressing the handle around a small tube of carbon steel. I don't need a lot of room, enough for a micro-kinetic field generator and a teensy-*tiny* Zero-point field module. Enough to power the kinetic field for a few hundred years. I need the kinetic field generator to give it weight. Titanium is incredibly light, even when bonded with tungsten carbide. With the kinetic field generator I can have it hit like a hundred pound weight. This is not a weapon I screw around with. Like my particle beam, it's lethal.

Kate is asking permission to teleport in. I had to ditch Epic's voice synthesizing. I love it, but I was having problems focusing on what he was saying. If something exploded at the moment he spoke he would have to say it again, or put it on my HUD anyways. I decided to stick with silent Epic. He could beep at me and get my attention if he needed to. Since I'm wearing the glasses I designed to hack with he can just scroll messages across my field of view.

"Uhm I'm not really—"

Pop.

"I brought you breakfast. I know you've been up all night and I thought you could use some food—wow, cool sword!"

I'm dead. Dead, dead, dead. She's an empath, it is going to take her exactly—

"Amelia..." she says in a naughty voice.

—that long to figure it out.

"What did you do?" she asks.

My face is flaming red, my ears are burning and I want to die. I spin my chair around and hide behind my computer pretending to go over the specs of the hilt.

"Spill girl, did you two—you know?"

Oh god, this couldn't be any worse.

"No, no we did not. Thank you very much." I say.

"You did something, it's like an emotional high in here."

"We kissed," I squeak out, "and there was some snuggling."

"Aren't you the cutest," she squeals. Kate is like this perfect woman. Pin-up model beautiful, eloquent, smart, and an empath. She can have any guy eating out of her palm. Literally and metaphorically. How she could possibly be excited about me having kissed someone is beyond me.

"You could knock me over with a feather," she says. Please leave, please! She isn't.

"Well I'm tired. I think I'll just go to bed," I say, knowing it won't work.

"Uh huh, come on Amelia, we're friends, a little girl talk won't kill you. Here, have a bacon, egg and cheese bagel from Ollie Vaughn's, they're to die for." I numbly take the sandwich knowing any second she is—

Her eyes light up and color rushes to her cheeks. She leans against my workbench for a second before she looks up at me, "Why didn't you tell me he is still here? He's dreaming about you, want to know what?"

I carefully open my bagel and nibble at it. She isn't wrong, it's the most delicious bagel I've ever tasted. I focus really hard on it while I bite at it in small parts. I know ignoring her won't make her go away, but I'm trying real hard.

"Oh fine, let me put up a wall for a second, his dreams are—intense."

Please stop talking! I take another nibble. After a moment she takes a deep breath and lets it out. She walks around to sit on my guest chair and takes out her own bagel.

After a few minutes of silence I feel like I can talk again. Maybe if I just completely ignore the fact Luke is sleeping in my bed she will too. It's not like we did anything wrong. It's just...

"I have walls against *his* emotions, not yours. Come on, Amelia, spill, you'll feel better," she says with a smile.

"Fine, we were kissing and then snuggling and I told him I like to watch Star Trek before bed and he actually said, 'Is that the one with Darth Vader?' I had to educate him. It's not my fault we fell asleep, fully clothed I might add, watching the second episode. I woke up a few hours ago to do some work on the sword. It isn't like I sleep a lot anyway."

"See, was that so hard?" she asks.

"Yes, yes it was. Would you like to see my sword?"

"I would love to."

I pop the last bit of buttery goodness in my mouth and click a few keys on the keyboard. The kinetic shield emitter I installed in the lab powers down enough for the sword to rest lightly on its display.

"Okay, pick it up and be very *careful*. You've seen Star Wars, right?"

"God, Amelia is everything about you this nerdy?"

I shake my head, "Geeky. Nerdy is when I start explaining the science behind it. Listen, the blade is what you would call—sharp. I don't want you lopping your arm off with it by accident."

She freezes her fingers on the hilt, "Is it really that sharp?"

I glance around the workshop for my pipe wrench, it's in the corner and I point, "Hand that to me, okay?" She does. I hold it up horizontally with an end in each hand.

"Now, carefully pick up the sword, line up the last few inches and give it a swing." I call it a sword because it is nearly four feet of titanium and carbon tungsten, but I decided to avoid the curved end. The blade is square with a thick ridge on top and the diamond coated blade on bottom. I don't really have a cross-guard, the blade ends and the round hilt begins. It's slightly larger than a sword would normally be, for me anyways. This way I can comfortably wield it while in my armor. It's not like I am going to do any fencing from my chair.

"Now would probably be a good time to tell you I am *slightly* stronger than your average woman," she says.

"Good, because it weighs about thirty pounds."

She wraps both her hands around the hilt and lifts the blade straight up, "Wow, yeah it does. Yet, it feels incredibly agile." She swings the sword back and forth a few times.

"Ahem," I nod to the wrench.

She places the square tip of the edge on top, lifts and comes down. The wrench comes apart like it was made in two pieces. The edges are perfectly smooth.

"Oh my *god*, you made this?" she asks.

"Yes I did," I answer with a grin, "The airport battle got me thinking about how Blade had this melee weapon and I simply could not come near her without getting hit."

"You didn't seem to have any problem with Tire-Iron, I noticed, You have to tell me sometime how you stopped a blow from an F5 strong man?"

"Science," I say to her.

"That's your answer for everything," she replies with narrow eyes. Carefully she puts the sword back on the pedestal. The display is made out of titanium too, but I'm pretty sure given time the sword would cut through it. The kinetic field emitter that makes it seem heavier, does the reverse when it is placed on its display. It ends up resting gently without the blade actually touching the alloy.

"This way I can have something for close combat and I don't have to go in with my fists. I can temporarily make my suits apparent strength extremely high—"

"—How high?"

"—High enough to catch an F5's fist with my hand," I say. My smile threatens to engulf my face when her jaw drops.

"That's how you stopped Tire-Iron's fist! How long can you maintain?"

"That level of strength? Only a few seconds. I can mimic F2 strength indefinitely. Which puts me around lifting a couple of tons at most."

There has been a hole in me since I was a little girl, and suddenly, hardly with me noticing, the hole is filling up. I've never had anyone to share this stuff with. Carlos is fun to hang out with, and he keeps me grounded, but it isn't the same. Kate understands. I have a best friend, I have a boyfriend—maybe—a place I belong. I never imagined this life. I started out wanting to find out about my parents, and now I have all this other stuff.

Before I know it the sun has been up for hours and Kate and I have been talking the whole time. She knows all the right things to get me to open up.

"You know, when I was twelve my powers expressed. They didn't have the test for it back then," she says to me.

"What happened?"

"I was in the seventh grade and one morning I felt *everything*. Every little piece of emotion everyone else felt, but I felt it all, felt it raw. I thought I was going crazy. I literally ran screaming from the school. My parents found me down by the waterfront... I was about to throw myself in when they came. I couldn't take it anymore. It was like I was everyone else and my mind was lost in an ocean of other people's emotions."

"How did you learn to control it?"

"There are special schools for people, places you can go and be you. Empaths are pretty rare, though, along with telepaths. There were maybe twenty other kids there with similar abilities. However, two years at brain school and I had a handle on it. I can put up shields and blocks, etc. It wasn't till later that the rest of my, um, powers came in." She waves her hand down her side and I realize she's talking about her looks.

"When that happened... I had to be locked away from everyone for almost a year." She gets this far away look in her eyes and I feel like an idiot. Of course not everyone here had a normal life. When I look at Kate all I see is the supermodel. I can be such a jerk.

"I'm sorry," I lean over and rest my hand on her leg, "I didn't know."

"It's tough all over, right? I had to spend three years in isolation learning to control my pheromones. A teenage girl with my powers is a disastrous combination. Lucky me by the time I learned to teleport it was all..."

"Ahem," Luke's voice comes from behind me.

"I'm sorry, I don't mean to intrude but, uh I wanted to take a shower and—" he fumbles for words and if I Kate and I weren't in the middle of a serious conversation, I'd be laughing.

"No, it's fine Luke," I say as I spin the chair around. I manage to wipe my eyes at the same time. "Um, can I see you later?"

"We do have a team exercises scheduled for today," he says with his drill sergeant voice. Terror floods me, did I misread everything? Didn't he like kissing me? Why wouldn't he want to see me again?

"Amelia, I'm joking, of course I want to see you again—socially. Would you like to have dinner with me tonight?"

I nod not trusting my words. He smiles, leans down and kisses me on the cheek. "Great, be ready at seven."

TWENTY-NINE

The hot water pouring over my head and shoulders feels incredible. My upper body aches from the strain of training. Six hours of team drills, practicing everything we might need. Luke was right to have us do it. We were lucky at the airport. Still, I'm sore as all hell. My suit isn't built to fly *and* carry someone. I had to figure out how to do it. It meant awkwardly holding someone in one hand while 'pushing' down with the flight stabilizer in the other. It ended up feeling like I did one-armed push-ups all day.

We practiced more than combat moves, we did tactics, and how to retreat in an orderly fashion. It was a long day, I liked it though. I got to be around Luke and with my mirrored faceplate he didn't see me giving him the goo-goo eyes all day. However, I did catch him looking at me more than once.

I turn the shower off and slide myself out onto the floor. It's much easier to be on the floor in the shower than to risk being on a bench or having someone here to help me. My shower is completely custom. The nozzle is only a few inches above me, I can easily reach it and adjust or detach it. I have all the soap and supplies I need. When I'm done I slide out and towel myself off. The mirror, sink, and everything else is on an adjustable counter I can raise or lower. Whether I'm on the floor or in my chair I'm covered.

Once I'm done there I use a step-like attachment to enter my wheelchair. I raise myself up one step at a time until I'm sitting in the chair and then I take the attachment off, easy-peasy.

Pop.

"I knew you were going to do that!" I holler at Kate. "Have you ever heard of knocking?"

"I wasn't in the neighborhood, but I wanted to help you get ready." She must have been at the gym, a light level of sweat glistens off her body. She's wearing boy shorts which hug her hips like they're painted on and a sports bra. Her muscles are incredibly toned and detailed, and her legs... the exact opposite of mine. She looks like she could run forever. Shapely, tone, agile. I glance down at my own, thin, emaciated, worthless. I wish she had waited until I was dressed instead of only wearing a towel.

"Oh honey, I'm sorry, It was thoughtless of me."

Empath, right.

"I—it's okay. You didn't—it isn't anything I didn't already know."

"Still, I pop in here wearing my workout clothes and I just—I didn't think. Forgive me?"

"Of course," I wipe my eyes with both hands. When did I become such a cry baby?

She wheels me out to the bedroom and gives me a brush to start on my hair. She pops out and almost right back again holding three bags. Two from a trendy place I would never shop at, and one is pink and is obviously from a lingerie store.

"I am not wearing that," I point at the pink bag.

"Listen, I'm not saying you have to undress for him, but trust me when I say, wearing this will make you *feel* sexy. When you feel it, you are sexy. Have a little faith I know what I'm talking about."

"Says the woman with the perfect body and mind control powers," I say skeptically.

"The truth is, Amelia, all women have mind control powers, it's just most never learn how to use them... I will show you and then the learner will become the master."

"Only a master of evil Kate," I laugh, "Okay, only because you nailed the quote. Show me."

A few hours later I'm in Luke's Ford F-150 driving down fifty-one to Camelback. He says he knows a great French place we can eat at. I love that he has a truck. A nice one too. He lifted my chair into the bed no problem. A perk of dating a man who can deadlift most cars is he won't have any trouble with my chair.

The interior of the truck is immaculate. There isn't even trash in the little receptacle. I reach over and flip on his radio, curious to see what kind of music he listens too.

Country, ugh, more country, country, *Cage the Elephant*. Score!

"We may not have overlapping taste in music," I say as the first notes of *Aint no rest for the wicked* plays. He smiles at me. His hand slides over and covers mine. This has got to be a dream. One I'm going to wake up from any minute... nope.

"You did great today in training. I thought Fleet was going to pee his pants when you hoisted him up in the air. For a guy who can run a couple of hundred miles an hour you would think flying would be no big deal," he says.

"Ha, yeah," I think about my next words carefully, "Luke, are we dating? I mean like, are we boyfriend and girlfriend?"

He focuses on the road for a moment, maneuvering his dark red pickup through some hairy traffic. I don't mind, he's wearing chinos and a tailored button-down blue shirt. I follow the line of his jaw down his neck to watch his muscles flow as the shirt strains slightly as he moves. I could seriously watch this all day.

"Do you want to be? I don't want you to feel pressure or anything, but I don't normally kiss women I don't want to be involved with."

"Can I tell you something?" Oh boy, I have no idea how to say this. Don't screw this up Amelia.

"Fire away," he says in typical marine fashion.

"You're the first guy who has ever wanted to date me, let alone kiss me," I stumble over the words. I had told Kate this and she suggested I tell him. Get it out of the way and clear expectations. I need to take it slow, she said he would understand.

"Are you saying you're a—"

"Someone who's never dated a guy before," I say with a little warning in my voice. Typical guy, the first thing he thinks is 'oh she's a virgin'.

"Amelia, you're twenty years old, a knockout and quite frankly one of the smartest people on the planet. How is it possible you've never dated before?"

I shrug, ignoring his obvious attempt at false flattery, "I'm dedicated. I cut everything out of my life I didn't need to have in order to be where I am. Honestly Luke, most guys don't even look once at a girl in a wheelchair, and I've been in it since I was six."

As I speak I hear a bit of anger in my own voice that surprises me. I thought I had come to terms with this a long time ago. It's easy, though, to come to terms with something when it isn't a possibility. Here, in this truck, it is.

"I would be honored to be your boyfriend, if you'll have me. Seriously though, no pressure."

I look at him carefully, "I don't want it to change our work dynamic. The team is really coming along and—"

"—You mean the dynamic where I yell at you and you slice me with some cutting remark?"

"Yeah, that one," I say fake punching him in the arm. It's like hitting a brick wall. I shake my hand. "Ow."

We drive the next few miles in silence. The sky fills with vibrant pinks and oranges as the sun continues its slow march toward the horizon. The western sky looks alive and on fire.

He gently guides the truck into a parking space outside a restaurant I'm positive he can't afford. Once he puts it in park he shuts the engine off and turns to me.

"Amelia, I'm not the smartest bulb in the bunch, I know this. If we were to speak of your intellect like my strength, then I'm you and you're me. I can't even imagine what it is like to have your wit, your imagination, to see the world the way you do? You make connections, you invent things, hell I'm just an ex-marine whose only asset is he can punch through steel. I have to be careful every single day not to hurt people. I'm desperate to control my emotions because my powers feed into my anger. The more my heart pumps the stronger I get. It's why I was in awe with what you did at the airport."

I turn to him as best I can and put my hand on his shoulder, "Luke, I... I'm not going to be patronizing, I know I'm smart—"

"—Genius—" he interjects.

"—Smart, and maybe not everyone can compare to that, but I don't think less of you because you can't do quadratic equations in your head. Honestly, it's refreshing to be around someone who *isn't* trying to prove he's smarter than me. I get in these *heated* debates with idiots at MIT who think everything in our world being a fractal at the molecular level is somehow a random coincidence and—" Shoot, I lost him, "Sorry, my point is you have your area of expertise and I have mine. I like that. It's clear lines of who can do what."

"I guess what I'm trying to say is... you're a catch. If you're willing to date me, then I am wholeheartedly on board," he says.

"Okay then, yes I—" he leans over and kisses me. It starts out gentle and sweet but quickly turns into something far more energetic. When we break the windows are fogged up and I'm breathing hard.

"Uh, we should eat," he says. A flush of red fills his face as he glances away from me. God he's cute.

"Alright then, muscles, retrieve my chair!" He smiles and throws a mock salute before he gets out of the truck. My phone vibrates in my clutch, which is a good reminder I need to shut it off. I pull it out and check the message fully expecting a teasing text from Kate. The truck rumbles and shakes. I put my hand on the dash and turn to tell Luke to take it easy with my chair. He's stumbling backward and I notice, every car is shaking. I hear glass break, someone screams and the asphalt splits open all over the parking lot. Earthquake? In Arizona? I manage to pull my seatbelt on and grab the handle in the roof and hold on for dear life. I close my eyes and my fear runs away with me. Please stop shaking!

There are so many simple things being paralyzed turns into a nightmare. This is certainly one of them.

After what feels like forever, the shaking stops. The door flies open and Luke is there. He slips his arms around me and holds me. I realize I'm crying. I hate being helpless. Add scared to it and I don't feel an abundance of control.

"You okay?" he asks.

"Yeah, yeah I'm fine." He doesn't let go, his arms wrap around me and I feel safe and secure. After a few moments I pat him on the back, letting him know he can let go. He holds on for a few more seconds before he does. He cups my chin and wipes some of my tears away with his thumb.

"Would it be terribly inappropriate to kiss you?"

"Please do," I whisper. After a few more minutes I'm starting to feel good again. Then I remember the phone. I pat him on the chest and he backs up a few inches.

"I think our date is going to be canceled," I say as I pull out my phone.

9.3 Earthquake in the Gulf of California. It's from Epic. He must have sent the message as soon as it happened.

It isn't natural. Something is moving in the bottom of the Gulf. The quake was near, but not on a fault. It isn't a subduction zone, there is no threat of tsunami.

I show the message to Luke. "We should probably get back to the office," he says in response.

"If there is something large enough to cause a massive quake in the Gulf, will the Mexican authorities be able to deal with it? I mean, they have super teams right?"

He shrugs, "I've never met them. We're not allowed across the border and as far as I know, they aren't either."

"I guess we'll find out," I say as he climbs in.

THIRTY

We're all in the break room of the HQ. Central is offline as is the teleportation elevator. Not that I would want to go through it after a massive Earthquake. Phoenix is two hundred miles away from the epicenter and we got shook up. The cities nearest in Mexico didn't fare well. I'm on the couch with Luke, he's holding my hand. Kate is sitting on the table, Pierre is floating in the air, and Tony is zipping back and forth from the kitchen and here to watch and eat. He's stocking up on calories and I can't say I blame him.

"They're going to call, right? Call and ask for help?" I ask.

Kate replies, "The tensions between our two countries are pretty high. Our idiot leadership with their nonsensical border policies aren't helping, then again neither are theirs."

Several news helicopters film the action below. Occasionally they will switch to talk about casualties or cities devastated but most are focused on what they are calling, *The Creature*. I honestly couldn't think of a better name. An hour after the Earthquake it emerged from the water. Its monstrous brown and gray head bubbles up from the surface a quarter mile from shore, when it's gigantic bloated body of scales, claws, and tentacles finally came forth, it was over a hundred and fifty feet tall.

It turns out, Mexico does have a super team. The entire world got to watch them die horrible deaths. Each one eaten by the monstrosity. Their army arrived shortly afterward, far too late to help those poor bastards. They were no more effective than the supers.

"It looks like the thing is turning north now. Yes we have confirmed course change. After a half hour of shambling East it is now turning north. The best estimate is it will hit the Arizona-US border in less than twelve hours. Our biologists are unable to explain the beast's enormous size, it must be a meta-lifeform of some kind."

I glance to the side and I notice everyone is looking at me. I shrug, "Why are you all looking at me, I'm not a biologist."

"If it is heading north from the Gulf then..." Kate didn't need to finish the thought.

"What's the call, Major Force?" Mr. Perfect asked from his floating lotus position. Luke looks around and I can see in his eyes he doesn't know what to do. He's a fantastic marine, and he can follow orders with the best of them, but coming up with his own stuff—it isn't his strong suit. Which begs the question, who put him in charge? Part of me thinks this entire team was set up to fail long before I ever arrived.

I squeeze his hand reassuringly, "I have an idea," I blurt it out before the silence drags on too long, "Why don't we suit up and at least go to the border. Epic can keep us updated on its progress. If the Mexican military can't or won't stop it, then at least we're in position."

"You did watch the entire Mexican national team be eaten, right?" Tony says quietly. I get he's scared. Hell I'm scared. How do you even fight something giant like it?

"I know you're all scared, I am too, but this *thing* is coming. If it gets into a city—thousands, millions, could die," I say.

"Won't the Feds send *The Brigade*?" Perfect asks.

"Maybe," Force says. For a moment it seems like he isn't going to say anything else, he just turns and looks out onto the desert behind us, "But, this is Arizona. They might arrive in time. They might not. Or maybe they're being ordered to hold back. If they come, they're in charge, but until then—this is our State."

That's more like it, he needed a few seconds to think things through. He looks to me and gives me a brief smile and his eyes twinkle.

"Suit up and be ready in thirty."

"We're not going to let Kate do her thing?" Tony asks.

Force shakes his head, "I want to be there and be rested when it arrives. If she ports us all there she'll be tired and we're going to need every edge. Fleet, Arsenal, I want you there ASAP. See if you can find us some advantage. Whatever you do, don't engage it, and don't cross the border." He looks sternly at both of us. We all break and head for our rooms. Fleet looks at me and grins, "Race you," and he's gone in a blur of motion. He's fast over open ground. I don't think I can catch him. Perfect and Kate run to their rooms. I grab Luke's arm as he stands.

"Come here," I whisper. He leans down and kisses me. I want it to last longer, but it can't.

THIRTY-ONE

"Epic, show me a map of the area it's likely to cross the border at?" I'm in flight cruising at ten thousand feet on a trajectory to the border. It's a one-hundred and twelve-mile trip. Epic puts up a slice of Arizona's south-western corner. On the American side there is a little town called—I can't stop myself from laughing—Lukeville! Oh Luke is going to get a kick out of this. On the Mexican side is Sonoyta. Epic pulls up their vital statistics. Lukeville is a 'city', and I use the term loosely, of a few hundred. Sonoyta has twelve thousand. They better be evacuating.

I'm cruising at three-fifty since I still haven't solved the overheating thruster problem. It isn't a mechanical problem with the thrusters, but a heat problem. As I approach Mach One the exhaust ports shoot past two-thousand degrees. When they're within five hundred degrees of three thousand, I have a problem. The suit will begin to break down at three thousand degrees. For now, I keep it under four hundred and I can fly for as long as I want. As long as I don't try to turn too much. The buffet at speed is incredible and one wrong move could have my arm pulled out of its socket. Which is why I have Epic lock the suit up so I'm not dripping sweat when I arrive with arms too sore to lift. On the bright side, my kinetic sheath works brilliantly and my sword stays firmly attached to my back.

Fleet pings me from a diner north of Lukeville. I check the clock, wow. He did it in thirteen minutes flat. I still have another nine minutes of flight time to go. I use that time to review the footage of the Mexican team. They're good, they work together, move as a unit but... it takes them out one by one. The thing has tentacles ending in sticky pods. Once it had its pods on them, it reeled them like a fishing rod. Ugh. Its mouth is full of shark's teeth. What the hell is this thing?

With its size and mass, hurting it will be a problem. Even at full power I doubt my particle beam could cut all the way through it. One of the Mexican supers had fire generation and it didn't even slow the thing down. I don't know what it's looking for, but it seems to have a direction in mind. Every once in a while it stops, and the pods waver in the air. After a few minutes it adjusts and starts going again.

Approaching Lukeville, I'm cutting velocity and freeing your hands for breaking maneuvers. When the speedometer falls under two-hundred MPH I bring up my hands and use the stabilizers as retro thrust to help slow us in.

"Epic, full sensor sweep." I see a problem. Even with a town of a few hundred, there should be cars lining the road. I thought for sure part of us being here would be to help with traffic and keep people moving to safety. There are three ways to go, North, south, and west, obviously no one is going to go south... I don't see a mass of headlights anywhere.

The ground comes up fast, forcing my attention to landing. The suit hits the asphalt outside the diner with an audible crack of concrete. I came in hot and spider webbed the ground. There is a blur of air and Fleet is standing in front of me.

"How come no one is evacuating?" I ask.

He shrugs, "The only people in the diner is a cook and a waitress. They're listening to it on the radio but there hasn't been a call for evacuation. The news is saying they're going to do air strikes on it and there isn't any need to worry."

Isn't any need to worry? They fired fifty-cals and anti-tank weapons at the thing and it didn't even slow down. What do they think a few air-to-surface missiles are going to do?

"Fleet, can you find the sheriff and alert him to the danger? I'm going to call this in."

He nods and vanishes in a blur. I notice little bolts of electricity wrap around him as he runs. I wonder if I hooked up a capacitor to him if he could power it?

Focus!

"Major Force, this is Arsenal, come in."

"What's your sitrep, Arsenal?"

Situation Report. Epic kindly translates for me.

"Bad, I think." I strike a pose and blast off into the sky. I have Epic put a beacon on my HUD showing me the border to keep me from accidentally crossing it. I use my stabilizers to try and hover in a forward motion to keep it down under fifty.

"I'm approaching the border now and there isn't anything happening."

"Good, the monster shouldn't be there for another eleven-odd hours and—"

"No, you don't understand," I interrupt him, "There isn't *anything* happening. No one is evacuating. Not from Lukeville, not from Sonoyta, nothing. Thirteen thousand people live in this region and there are only three roads out. One of which leads to the creature. These roads should be packed with traffic." I'm trying not to sound desperate but I think I'm failing. Thousands of people are asleep in their homes less than a mile from me. An imaginary line on a map is the only thing keeping me from helping them.

Luke must have forgotten he had an open mic, I hear him swear for a solid thirty seconds.

"I'll contact Central and find out what the emergency plan is."

Like *that* will help. Something is better than nothing, at least.

"Good, tell them air strikes are a waste of time, too. There isn't anything in any arsenal powerful enough to hurt this thing. El Fuego, was an F5. He could generate fire over two thousand degrees hot. If he couldn't hurt it, Paveways and Cluster bombs aren't going to scratch it."

Please understand, Luke, make them listen!

"I'll pass it on to Central. Out"

When the line clicks dead I form a plan. It's obvious outside help is going to be insufficient.

"Epic, is there a civil defense siren in Lukeville?"

Searching—yes. It isn't currently operative according to the mayor's email to the Army Corps of Engineers dated thirteen years ago.

"Good thing I'm an engineer. Show me."

THIRTY-TWO

"They want us to assist in the evacuation of Americans, but our standing orders are in effect. We don't cross the border," Luke tells me over the radio. There in a SUV heading down here and it will arrive in an hour. Apparently the Hover cycles are in for their annual maintenance. Another coincidence?

"Is Central sending us any assistance? The California team could be here in twenty minutes on their vehicles." I tell him while I pull a wire from the civil defense siren and strip the plastic housing. Doing detailed work in the suit isn't as easy as I thought it would be.

"I've contacted the governor's office and let them know they should consider calling a state of emergency. Without it though, we have to make do. The national guard is on the way, and they were confident the Brigade would show up."

Damn, this would be a perfect time to find out some info on them... but...lives first. When did saving lives and being a hero become more important than finding out what happened to my parents?

"Fine, I'm sure they will be awesome," I can't keep the vitriol from my voice.

"Amelia, I know how you feel about—"

"Are they going to call off the air strikes?" I didn't want to talk about it. Not now. I need to focus. Thirteen thousand people. Men, women, and children were all counting on me getting this outdated, rusted, piece of crap working!

"No, the Pentagon rep told me they are one-hundred percent confident they will work," he said. I could hear the man who wanted to have faith in his government. He knew I was right and the conflict in his voice says so.

"At least it shouldn't hurt anything. Okay, see you when you get here. Park at the diner." I disconnected the call.

The wiring is too old. If I hook it to the suit I will blow it all up, I need something stronger than a car battery but not too powerful.

"Fleet, you find the Sheriff yet?"

"Negative. The police station is closed. At this point I might have to go door to door," he says.

"Awesome, come to m—"

A blur of motion flashes and Fleet is grinning at me.

"I notice electricity flashes around you when you move. Is it you or is it static electric build up?" I ask. His blank stare tells me it's static.

"Good, take your glove off," he does, "and hold this." I hand him the power cable to the siren.

"I always thought the little lightning bolts were because I'm fast," he said with a grin.

"They are, sorta," I kneel down and pull the baseplate off, "it's called 'electron affinity' as you move through the air, electrons from the particles in the air, like dust, are attracted to you. Your protons like electrons more than the dust in the air does. As you move at super-speeds the electrons begin to collect on your surface. You don't feel it because it's you. However, if you were to run without your fancy suit, and the weather conditions were hot and dry, the first person you touched would feel it."

"How much would they feel it?" asked Fleet.

"Like a Taser. Start moving your left arm in circles, about six inches radius should do." Within a few seconds his arm blurs out of existence. The noise it makes isn't dissimilar to a helicopter. Bolts of electricity leaped around him and into the power cable. The familiar keen of the civil defense siren warbles to life.

"That's loud," Fleet says. The electricity he generates powers up the siren to full strength. It sounds like an old time air raid siren.

I grinned, "I know. Do this for fifteen minutes, I'm gonna see if it has an effect." I launch into the air in a swirl of dust. I probably should have moved away from him before taking off. Whatever, the dust I kicked up will help.

At a thousand feet I slow to an unstable hover. Up here, Epic registers over fifty decibels on the siren. Perfect. I switch to thermal as I scan the surrounding countryside. Blooms of heat are coming on everywhere. I look to Sonoyta, same thing. A wave of relief washes over me.

"Epic, I know I'm asking a lot, but you need to find every active device with a wi-fi or cellular signal and you tell them to evacuate any direction but south."

This will require much of my processing power. There are seven different cell companies and Internet providers I will have to access.

"Do it, I can manage."

Affirmative.

While Epic does his thing I head over to the center of Lukeville. The place may be quiet but there has to be a police officer on duty somewhere. I do a slow circle of town with my eyes peeled for him.

All the residential lights are on now. There are even some people coming out of their homes. I spot him, he's driving a beat-up old Bronco through the center of town. He parks in front of the small police station. I kick in the jets and I'm over him in a few seconds. He looks up and his face goes white as I land a few feet from him.

"Sheriff, my name is Arsenal, I'm with the Diamondbacks." I tell him. He's off guard and I notice his hand moving to his pistol.

"Sheriff, I'm bulletproof, please don't endanger anyone with ricochets." Now I have his attention.

"Sorry ma'am, it's just—I ain't ever seen anyone fly before," as he speaks he takes his hat off and runs his hands through his thinning hair. He has to be in his fifties. He's stayed in decent shape and I can see traces of military in him, he has the walk.

"Are you why the civil defense siren is waking everyone up?"

"Yes, there is a creature heading directly here. We need to evacuate the town." I try to sound authoritative. My synthesized voice is strong and sure.

"Creature you say? How big a threat could it be that we need to evacuate the entire town?"

As he asks Epic finishes his work. The man's cell phone beeps and the emergency broadcast system activates every phone, computer, wireless TV, and game console within fifty miles.

"This is a notification of an Emergency. All residents in, or near Lukeville, Arizona should evacuate to the north. This is not a test." The voice goes in a loop after it finishes.

"Well done, Epic. You've earned your keep today!"

Considering how inexpensive I am, you aren't saying much. This is what I get for programming him to learn.

"All right then, I'll get all the deputies on duty and we'll keep the highway moving."

I give him our teams radio frequency for him to call us if he needs us. After he goes inside I switch over to Fleet.

"They're evacuating we can end it." The siren dies down and I hear Fleet's voice over the radio, "I need some food, running is easier than what you had me do."

I check the clock, ten hours to go. I ignite the jets and I'm back at a thousand feet. I do a little pirouette to see all around. The area surrounding Lukeville is alive with activity. I check Sonoyta—not nearly enough.

"Were you not able to send the message to the Mexican town?"

Different systems in a different country. There is no possibility of doing it without being caught. If I cross the border to warn people it's an act of war, as sure as if the Army crossed it. If Epic hacks their system it is an international crime and will likely be traced back to him.

Great. Maybe the team will have an idea when they get here. One way or the other, we're evacuating Sonoyta.

THIRTY-THREE

In the remaining time before the team arrived a lot happens. The sheriff rouses all his deputies and starts organizing the evacuation. Cars filled with families, belongings, and pets start to trickle onto the road heading north. Every light in the county is on. Will it be in time? Not for Sonoyta if they don't follow suit.

The black SUV carrying the rest of the team pulls up next to me in the parking lot of the Diner. Fleet is inside stuffing his face with ice cream and anything else he can find calorically-dense enough to last him. I fill them in on what's happening on both sides of the border. The clock on my HUD shows less than nine hours to go.

"We can't do anything about Sonoyta, it isn't our problem," Luke says. Domino and Perfect have the decency to look uncomfortable. I know Fleet agrees with me. We should cross the border, find their police and warn them to evacuate.

"Surely there's an exception to the rules we can use? Some 'in case of emergency' clause? I don't think the ambassadors in the nineteen-sixties when the Borders Super Powers Treaty was signed, ever envisioned giant sea monsters attacking. Can you at least call Central and ask them to put in a request?"

His eyes cloud over when I ask him. What is going on with this stupid organization? I thought it was me, but it has only gotten worse. At every turn they set us up to fail. Not enough team members. Not enough support. Sending us places we can't possibly hope to survive. Of course they go silent now.

"They've forwarded the Federal Governments orders to us, and it is all they will say. The Arizona militia is to assist with evacuations, and no more. The Brigade will be on-site at oh-eight-hundred to deal with the creature if joint air strikes fail. It's all I get out of them, sorry Arsenal."

Oh-eight-hundred, huh? About an hour before the creature is scheduled to arrive.

"Fine, what's the play then?" I have my own plan forming. If it works, Sonoyta is saved. If it doesn't, I will likely spend the rest of my life as a fugitive... cause I'm sure as hell not going to surrender the armor to stand trial.

Luke goes into leader mode, this is a straight up problem he can deal with. "Fleet, start checking the houses farthest out, maybe a mile, and make sure they're aware of the danger and assist in helping anyone who needs help." Fleet nods and in a blur of motion, is gone.

"Domino, assist Fleet as needed, you can 'port around and be our backup. If anyone needs assistance you can help."

"Understood," she says.

"Perfect, you and I are on traffic duty. I'll station myself at the entrance to the highway to keep people moving in an orderly fashion. I want you in the intersection where the roads meet. Keep accidents from happening and help as needed."

"I'm on it, oh illustrious one," he says with a too-wide perfect grin. He wiggles his fingers and the flying carpet he confiscated from Jadoo the now brain-dead, appears and he leaps on. He takes off into the night with a flap of snapping fabric.

"I didn't know we could loot the enemy," I say casually.

"He told the authorities it was some sort of magical artifact and it would only be safe with him," Domino says in the tone of voice she reserves for telling jokes.

"What do you want me to do, Force?"

Luke looks around at the city for a moment before speaking, "Can you be our eye in the sky? Let us know if any hot spots flare up or if anything unexpected happens."

"Sure, not a problem." I put my arms down in flight form. Before I kick off the thrusters he puts a hand on my shoulder. Domino wanders away talking on her radio to give us a moment.

"I know you want to help those people, I do too." He looks at my faceplate, I have it slide back to see his eyes with mine.

"We can't let them die," I say.

"You told me once you have stealth on your suit," he says.

"Yeah..."

"We don't have to report everything..." He nods and holds my gaze for a second, "Good luck." We can't kiss, my armor is in the way, but oh how I wish we could.

"You too," I reply and seal up the armor. He turns away as I blast off into the sky. Message received, do what I have to do. I'm glad he's on board with it. I can't believe I didn't think of it first.

"Epic, engage stealth systems."

My HUD switches from light green to dark blue. Things like radar reflection, heat, and altitude all become more prevalent, since those are the readings directly related to stealth. I have to keep my speed down as I bank us over at two hundred feet and put the compass squarely on 'S'.

It only takes a few minutes and I'm crossing the border.

You are now in violation of international law regarding the illegal border crossing of powered individuals.

"Really? You're going to tell me this, Mr. Illegal AI?"

Technically, only the construction, not the existence of AI is illegal. Yet another crime you've committed. lol

I laugh. Epic's read on my emotional state is spot on and a little laughter clears my head.

"Thanks, buddy."

Anytime.

"All right, now, how do we convince these people to evacuate?" There were a few who heard the siren and paid attention. The vast majority are still in their homes.

"Epic, if we were to use my audio synthesizers and crank up the decibels, could we fly around and broadcast an evacuation order?"

Calculating... affirmative. I've located footage on the Internet with acceptable audio of a man speaking Mexican-Spanish ordering people to evacuate. Cleaning it up... adding authority... reticulating splines...

"You made that last one up." I say, trying not to laugh.

Ready.

"Do it."

I pull up to three hundred feet to give it the most spread. A loud, clear voice emanates from my armor.

"By authority of the governor of Sonora and the president of Mexico, all citizens are ordered to evacuate to the north, west or east. The American border is available. Do not travel south."

There's a pause and it repeats again. I complete one full circuit of the town and lights are starting to come on. Excellent.

Fast movers incoming. Elevated radar signals. Drop to two-hundred feet.

I do without waiting for an explanation. A deep rumble echoes from the sky to the north. Above me. Flying at Mach 1, are a pair of F-22 Lightnings, ultra fast, ultra high-tech fighters. They pass silently above followed by their noise a few seconds later. Only two. Did the Pentagon not watch the same video we did? The presence of the fighters isn't a complete waste, they add legitimacy to my broadcast. Lights all over the little town spring to life and within a few minutes cars are streaming in all directions but south. Excellent.

Now we have to hope the civilians evacuate in time and we can somehow defeat a giant monster.

It's all downhill from here.

THIRTY-FOUR

The air strikes failed, of course. The team and I are on the border, watching this *thing* roll through south Sonoyta. I can only imagine the casualties if we hadn't convinced them to evacuate since no evacuation order ever came from the US or Mexico. The creature is a hundred feet tall and twice as wide. It has flailing tentacles and pods all over its body. It 'walks' by undulating thousands of knobs on its underside. For something big enough to fill a football stadium, it moves pretty fast. Watching it move is almost as bad as listening to it. A cacophony of squeals and barks, enough to sound like a confused mass of seals and eels.

Epic estimates it's thirty minutes from crossing the border.

A loud roar catches our attention as a VTOL swings by overhead. The wings spin up pointing the engines down as the ship comes to rest a few hundred feet away from us.

They have arrived.

The side door opens and Captain Freedom exits first. His red, white, and blue jumpsuit is made with muted colors. He wears a trench coat over it and protects his face with what looks like a hockey mask painted with the American flag. Comanche follows him. I don't know a lot about him. Epic lists him as a F5 and extremely dangerous. He can produce focused ion beams from his eyes. After him is Torque, a young Latino who is new to the team. He can create force fields and manipulate them in interesting ways. Mariposa flutters out of the plane to take flight above the team. She floats aloft on delicate looking butterfly wings. She is also a telepath which makes her a natural at logistics and communications. The last person to exit the plane is Behemoth. If there is one, truly, scary individual on the team, it's her. Six four with a physique which looks carved from stone. Her eyes are black pits radiating hate all around her. The ground sinks slightly as she steps on to it and the plane rocks up on its suspension once she's off.

"They're—impressive," Perfect says over the comms. It's hard not to be intimidated by them. They're a full on team with an unlimited budget and years of experience. They're also some of the most powerful supers in the world. I've heard Behemoth's max strength is unreadable, there isn't anything heavy enough to test her against.

The four of us, me, Force, Domino, and Fleet are standing together like herbivores trying to scare off the predators. Captain Freedom spots us and heads our way. The rest of his team hangs back.

"Epic, full sensors, I want to know as much as possible about all of them." I watch my HUD light up as my electronic warfare suit comes online. Everything from sonic vibrations to light reflection is being recorded.

"Major Force?"

Oh god. I just got his name... I thought it was his rank in the marines. Thankfully no one can hear me snicker.

"Captain," Force replies with a crisp salute.

"Yeah, whatever. Have you handled the civilian evacuation?" I can tell Luke is a little let down by Freedom's dismissal of his honorific salute.

"Yes sir, all civilians have been evacuated, on both sides of the border."

Freedom stiffens, "You didn't cross the border, did you?"

"No, sir."

I'm not sure what to think about Freedom. I don't like him, I know that. He's rude to Luke, for one thing. There is also a certain jadedness to him. Maybe because he's older or maybe because he's a jerk, I don't know.

"Your people did well, pack it up and head back to Phoenix." He doesn't wait for acknowledgment he turns around and walks back to his group. I can feel the astonishment around me.

"Force we're not—"

"I don't think—"

"This is some bulls—"

Everyone is talking at once and I can see the war in Luke. He wants to obey, but he knows Arizona is *our* state. I make the decision for him.

"We'll hang back if you don't want our help. Once you've all died exposing its weakness, I'm sure we'll be able to take it down." There goes my mouth again, I really should look into sealing it or something.

Freedom stops dead in his tracks. I've hit a nerve. Mariposa snaps her head over to look at us, she must have felt his sudden mood change.

He turns around and storms right up to me. I'm only five eight in the armor, it isn't like it's hard to tower over me. However, I'm not intimidated in the least by him. Angered, yes.

"This is our show. We don't need interference from local *hicks* to screw us up."

The creature is approaching the tail end of the civilians. It appears to have picked up speed as it sensed food. I'm recalculating...

"How many are likely in its path given the new data?"

Hundreds.

"Are you listening, Diamondbacks? Go home," he says in one final explosive breath. My team doesn't move.

"Force, the thing has picked up speed and it will catch up with the tail end of the civilians. Hundreds will be killed."

"That's not our problem, it's up to the Mexican government to protect her people," Freedom spits out. He's angry, but I feel like he isn't angry with me so much as the situation. Suddenly a theory rushes through my main like a train. I glance at the creature, then at the Brigade. They've been ordered to stand down. It makes so much sense now. Cat-7 wants the creature for itself. If even a part of it is on the Mexican side of the border, there will be a custody battle. The biology of that thing could be worth billions.

"Arsenal, I—I don't know what to do," Luke says.

"I do. Fleet go move as many people out of the path of the creature as possible. Domino, once he's there, port to him and start moving people out. Perfect, fly over as fast as you can, maybe you can use your," I can't believe I'm about to say this, "magic to wall off people if they can't get away, or move cars or what not. Force, I'm going to carry you with me, I'll drop you off a few hundred feet in front of it. Build some sort of barricade, car, signs, hell, knock down buildings if you need too, anything to slow it down." They all nod.

"I'm ordering you and your people to stand down," Freedom says. His anger has vanished and now he sounds almost... unperturbed.

"I'm not a big order follower, just ask Force," I say.

"Some of us do." He nods at me and turns to walk away. Was it all a game? Did he blow up to push us into action? If he was ordered not to cross the border—then this is his way of getting those people help.

"Diamondbacks, do Arizona proud," I say. Fleet blurs and he's gone in a trail of dust as he runs toward the border. Perfect flies off on his carpet, it's going to take him a little while to arrive. Domino hangs back so she can—*pop* and she's there. Good for Fleet.

"Alright handsome, it's you and me." I hold out my hands to Luke. He takes my wrist and we lock together.

"Ame—Arsenal, thank you," he whispers to me.

"You might want to hold off on the 'thank you' until after we're not dead or in jail."

This is going to be rough. With one hand holding him we're going to have to make up in speed what we lack in stability.

"Full power burn, go!"

THIRTY-FIVE

I let Luke go as I pass by a group of people whose cars were stuck together. I'm confident he can square it away. Fleet blurs in and out moving people and things forward. I hear the *pop* of Domino teleporting to add to it all. Now to deal with the creature. It crushes everything in its path, trees, cars, houses alike.

I pull up to hover a hundred feet in front of it. Long tentacles ending in pods wave in the air. I don't see any eyes or other sensory input. It's a mass of sponge-like material crammed with a hundred different parts of sea creatures. Its maw is twenty feet wide, I get a good look as it opens to breathe. It sucks in a huge breath, enough to cause trees to bend toward it. Just like we saw on TV, the maw is full of row after row of shark teeth. What sort of nightmarish hell did this thing come from?

"Epic are we clear yet?"

Negative. The efforts of the team will not save everyone. They need an additional six minutes.

Six minutes? This thing may be the size of small cruise ship, but I should be able to distract it for six minutes. Okay then. I'm still hovering. There's a pit of fear in me and it's freezing me in place.

Focus! I can do this. I take a couple of deep breaths and shake my hands. One giant monster against one very small, frightened woman. What could possibly go wrong?

I burn sideways and do a quick loop. It all looks the same. The only variation in texture is around the mouth and at the bottom where it moves along the ground. How to get its attention?

"Combat HUD, Epic." The HUD switches to an angry red. Weapons status and power levels, all one-hundred percent, for now. As I fly around it I circle in closer. Once I'm behind it I point my right arm, hand down, at it. The particle beam lights off. I'm fifty feet away, which is not optimal range for the beam. It slices through the thing spilling orange guts and bits as I drag the hyper-accelerated silicon particles across it. I burn across ten feet of its hide with no effect.

Up in the air above it again and—crap, it didn't even notice.

"Epic, if I was at point blank range would the particle beam do more damage?"

Based on all available data, you could fire the particle beam until the suit ran dry and not significantly hurt it. One minute until I estimate the first civilian is caught.

I redline my thrusters and I fly right at it. Banking hard I grunt from the g-forces. In the middle of my arc I let loose with a full power IP cannon blast. I don't expect it to do a lot but I can hope. I need a few minutes for the particle cannon to recharge. The Ion Pulses dissipate against its hide. If it noticed, it didn't show. I wish I had actual grenades in my launcher because I don't think pods are going to—

I grunt as a giant tentacle shoots out at me and slaps me in midair. The kinetic shielding screams at me. *Fifteen percent.*

I get a real close look at the pod. It has suckers on it and they're spitting an orange juice at me. It doesn't have any pressure and since the shield held they're two feet away. Time to test my new toy. I reach behind me and draw the sword. I feel it hum as the ZPFM kicks in to make it weigh far more than it does. I grip it with both hands, relying on Epic to manage the thrusters for a second. I swing in a downward cleave—the black blade slices through the tentacle with ease. Viscus orange liquid sprays out of the severed end.

The thing grinds to a halt. Its mouth opens and a deafening keen fills the air. Windows shatter, car alarms blare, people two hundred feet away fall to their knees holding their bleeding ears.

"Reroute all available power to the shields, I need them recharged fast!" I see the numbers start climbing but it isn't fast enough. I turn to face the thing and kick my feet out slightly to put me moving more east than north. I need it to follow me. A pod shoots out at me from below. The blade intercepts it and cuts it down. Another from the right, I cut it too. Above me and—

I'm hit again. Alarms blare as the HUD flashes at me. Kinetic shields are down. They're going to need at least thirty seconds to charge. Less if I land. I manage to right myself in the air. The thrusters land me gently on the roof of a building. It looks like a church. The creature is thoroughly focused on me now—fantastic. Its ginormous form shuffles toward me on spindly, sponge-like legs. I can only see them now as it crests a small hill. The rest of the time they're hidden

"Domino, Fleet, go help Arsenal and—"

"No," I scream overly loud, "Civilians first. Once they're clear we fall back and come up with a plan." I don't listen for their acknowledgments, I have too much to handle in front of me.

A barrage of tentacles come slashing at me. I do my best to intercept them with the blade. I cut one, spin, slash another. Orange ichor splashes around me.

Toxic atmosphere forming, switching to internals.

I thought I smelled something acrid. Is the orange stuff acid? The wooden wall of the church steeple breaks my horizontal trip. One of the pods hit without me seeing it. I crash against the ground thirty feet away. Rolling and flopping I come to a halt.

"Epic, where's the sword?" There wasn't any way to hold on while I was spinning. He pings it on my HUD and I run for it. I scoop it up and engage thrusters. This thing is too big to hurt. Even chopping off its pods is only pissing it off.

"Civilians?"

"All clear," Force comes back.

"Okay, I'm heading back your way to re—"

My kinetic shield howl as alarms sound all over the place. One of the tentacles wraps around my leg. Another pod slams into my side and it sticks. Thick goo sprays all over my armor followed by little suckers with hooks trying to dig into my armor. If I were flesh, even strong flesh...

"Oh my god I know what this thing does and why the Mexican team couldn't break free. They were dead the moment these pods attach. They paralyze you with this goop they secrete on the outside and then inject your body with acid and start 'drinking' in the melting flesh." I want to vomit as I say it. Knowing it, and seeing it up close sends a shiver down my spine. Lucky for me my military grade alloys aren't easily hurt by acid. *Maybe* if I was to sit in a cauldron of boiling hydrochloric acid for an hour it would hurt.

It's desperately trying to reel me in like a fish on a hook.

"Arsenal, break free!" It's Luke yelling for me.

Oh crap. I have an idea, but it is going to suck.

"Trust me," I say as I feel myself flying through the air. "Epic, lock me up and keep pumping power to the kinetic shields!"

Are you sure this is wise?

"Hell no!"

I hit something soft then I'm bucking around. My HUD flashes each time the thing brings its mouth down on me. My shields drop rapidly, but they do hold.

"Ars...l, d. you c..y? ...enal? Amei..., get ... of ..ere!"

The thing's hide must be playing havoc with the radio. No matter. I don't need to hear them for what I'm about to do. This is totally crazy but I'm the only one who can do it. I doubt even Behemoth could survive those acid spitting suckers. Even if she could, she'd certainly be paralyzed by the goo.

Kilopascals on my suit increase a hundred fold. If it wasn't for me being locked up I would likely be crushed. Rigid though, with each piece supporting the next, and with the internal kinetic field working, it's more like a bumpy ride. The pressure comes off and I'm falling. I bounce a few times as I make my way down.

"Epic, external lights, please?"

The LED's flash to life, I have them all over the suit and I stand out like a beacon. Everything is orange and I'm surrounded by the viscous orange blood/acid.

The internal atmosphere ticks over to fourteen minutes. I don't have a ton of time.

Amelia, even if you were to fire the particle cannon full power, this thing is too vast to hurt. Even from the inside.

"I know, unlock me." My limbs jerk free. I reach behind and pull my sword off. I'm ever-thankful I didn't try to use a mechanical sheath. Once the two kinetic fields lock together it's like pulling a magnet apart. An electromagnet with an infinite power supply.

"Charge the particle cannon." The meter starts rising on the beam weapon.

Amelia, what are you doing?

At twenty percent I fire. The particle cannon cuts through the hilt of my sword cleanly, exposing the two pieces of technology inside. My kinetic field generator and miniature Zero-Point Field Module. I wish I could work in a dry environment, but we're dealt the hands we're dealt. The housing for both is in titanium, it won't last very long under this. However, I don't need it to last long.

They're already connected together which makes this much easier than it otherwise would be.

"Epic, access the kinetic field and invert it. I want to compress the ZPFM with the energy from the ZPFM."

...I don't know what will happen if you do this.

"I do, the ZPFM will compress and release more energy, compressing it more, until there is no room for the atoms to compress and..."

You're going to create a supernova.

"Yes, once the heat reaches a point the housing can no longer sustain or acid breaches... boom. Hopefully it will be a very small supernova."

I sit the two pieces down and stand up.

Initiating. We should flee.

"Yep." I pick the sword up and hold it above me like a spear pointed straight up, "Full burn, now!" The acid boils around me as the thrusters kick in. The soup is thick. The sword hits something but I slice right through it and—free! The air hisses around me as the acid on my suit comes in contact. I tune it out.

"We need to get everyone out of the blastzone right now," I yell over the radio.

"Arsenal, you're alive!" Domino comes on the comms.

"Blastzone?" Mr. Perfect asks.

"Yes, one mile at least. Move it."

It's back on me; I guess I pissed it off enough. I turn south and start leading it away. The massive thing turns on its access and starts chewing up ground as it comes after me.

Amelia, there is a temperature build up inside it. I glance at our velocity, seventy-five, just enough to stay airborne and keep this thing interested.

"Fire a pod straight up." *Puff.*

"Full burn, maximum thrust. We need to hit Mach one." The roar of my jets threatens to shake me apart. I grab the pod as we pass it and stick it to my chest.

"We're clear of the blast zone," Force says.

"Awesome, Luke, if I don't make it—thanks."

The world turns into a massive globe of light. My HUD sparks and vanishes. A wall of force a hundred times stronger than a tsunami hits me. I'm thrown in a million different directions at once.

"Lock up," I manage to yell. Epic obeys a moment before I would have broken something. The vertical G's are too much. Blackness creeps in from the sides dimming my vision an inch at a time until all I see is black.

THIRTY-SIX

"Amelia," I can hear someone calling my name but I can't see anything. Where am I? The world is nothing but blackness and silence. Except for this one insistent voice shouting my name. Louder and louder until my head hurts from the yelling.

"Quiet," I manage to mutter. Then it all came back. I hear someone groaning and then I realize it's me.

"Did we win?" I ask the shouting voice.

"You did it, Amelia, you did it. A single line of light pierces my vision and I realize why everything is dark, My faceplate is covered in grime and the single line of light is Luke doing his best to wipe the gunk from it.

I move my arms to test them, they seem to work.

"Epic?"

Nothing.

"Epic?" I can't keep the edge of panic out of my voice. I can make out Luke's smiling face as he finishes scrubbing the gunk off.

"I can't connect to Epic," I tell him. He cocks his head to the side glances down at my armor.

"You have some exterior damage, a crap ton of pitting and scorch marks. Maybe your power cells have been damaged?"

Power, I must have generated a crazy powerful emp. Even shielded I bet it took down some systems.

On cue my faceplate lights up. Lines and lines of data scrolls past my screen as Epic runs a full diagnostic scan. When the last line flashes by my HUD blinks rapidly several times before resolving to the familiar blue glow.

Sorry, Amelia. I had to shut down a microsecond before the EMP hit and I didn't have time to explain.

"I can't see your face, is everything okay?" Luke asks me.

"Everything's great, Epic is back."

"Are you okay?"

All systems are functional, albeit in low power mode. I'm afraid the suit isn't combat ready. Though, sustained flight is possible.

"Awesome."

With Luke's help I shakily pull myself up to a standing position. He wraps his big arms around me and I find myself wishing I could take the armor off so he could hold me.

"God, Amelia, I thought I lost you," there is something disconcerting about a man his size shaking with tears in his eyes. I do my best to return the hug.

"It's okay, Luke, I'm fine. Really."

We stay that way for a few minutes before the rest of the team shows up. Domino and Mr. Perfect appear out of thin air and Fleet arrives in a blur. I've never been so happy to see people in my whole life. I can't stop the tears as we all hug.

"Sone of a gun, we did it," Fleet says as we all hug.

I want this moment to go on forever. My heart sings from the proximity of my friends. Kate flashes me a huge smile as she glances at Luke who hasn't looked away from me since I stood up.

"Okay, Diamondbacks. Let's go home," Luke finally says.

"Who's hungry, because I say we take over an Outback and party like it's 1999," Mr. Perfect says with his cocksure smile.

"My treat," I add, "But I need about a hundred hours of sleep.

"Amen to that," Kate chimes in.

Epilogue

I had to let Epic take the wheel for the trip home. Exhaustion seeped into me and somewhere over southern Arizona I fell asleep. It was a short-lived nap, however. Alarms buzzed alerting me to ignite my retros to slow down. Epic can lock the suit up and even steer it a little, but not control it outright.

I groan as I lift my arms, they feel like lead weights. The thrusters hit and spin me around. The boot jets kick in and slow me down enough to only crunch the gravel on the roof the of the HQ when I hit. I stagger, more than walk, the few feet to the elevator. I would have used my private entrance but I'm too tired to aim and would likely have hit the wall, not the window.

The team is still a half hour away when the armor comes off. I'm drenched in sweat from the work. The outside of my armor is blackened and pitted from both the acid and the explosion. I can fix the paint job, the pitting though... it might be time to move to a MKII.

I can't think about it, though, too tired. I strip off my interface suit and groan as I flop on the bed. A shower would do wonders but I am too tired to care.

I gaze up at the ceiling willing sleep to take me, but there is an incessant buzzing keeping me from going over. I hit the bed in frustration.

"What?"

I glance at the nearest TV screen, Epic has it lit up with a picture of a bunker of some kind. Underneath it he says, *I've found your parents.*

FROM THE AUTHOR,

Never fear true believer, there will be a book two, or a Mark II. Arsenal was an interesting book for me to write. Numerically it is my fifth novel but the first one released under my own name. The majority of the story and the structure came together in nine days. As you can imagine, that is pretty unusual.

I've wanted to write superhero fiction for a long time but I wanted to write something a little different. Don't get me wrong, I will read Spidey all day long. However, I wanted to create someone who wasn't just a cookie cutter hero. Enter: Amelia. Super-smart, quick witted and wheelchair bound. I did a lot of research about that. I didn't want it to be lip service, but I also didn't want it to be the subject of the story. Nor did I want her to 'invent' a cure. She never will. Flying around as Arsenal is the closest she will get. I love the world and the characters and I hope it sells well enough to justify my return.

If you did like the book, please consider leaving a review, it is incredibly helpful to authors. You can also check out my web page and sign up for my mailing list. I do giveaways all the time.

WWW.JEFFERYHHASKELL.COM

Shock washes over me. He's found them? Now? How? What... I don't know what to do.

They're in Boston. The latest data dump from our backdoor shows them arriving there fourteen years ago. I know where they are Amelia... They're alive. Those three little words lifted my spirits to new heights.